MW00466865

A LION'S MATE

A LION'S PRIDE #13

EVE LANGLAIS

Copyright © 2020/2021 Eve Langlais

Cover Art by Yocla Designs © 2020/2021

Produced in Canada

Published by Eve Langlais

http://www.EveLanglais.com

E-ISBN: 978 177 384 1984
Print ISBN: 978 177 384 1991

All Rights Reserved

This book is a work of fiction and the characters, events and dialogue found within the story are of the author's imagination and are not to be construed as real. Any resemblance to actual events or persons, either living or deceased, is completely coincidental.

No part of this book may be reproduced or shared in any form or by any means, electronic or mechanical, including but not limited to digital copying, file sharing, audio recording, email and printing without permission in writing from the author.

PROLOGUE

Warning: The beginning, like many a famous animated movie, starts with the death of a parent. If you want to skip it, head to Chapter One. If you want to experience the event that shaped the heroine, then continue reading.

THE BEAR MUST HAVE BEEN HIDING amongst the icy pillars. They filled the room, liquid crystal sentinels, some of them wide enough to hide a rather large ursine.

They should have smelled it, and yet, there were so many scents. The moist steam hinting of something acrid. Fetid with a bit of rot.

It lumbered into view suddenly, its fur more a

dingy gray than white, clumped on its mottled body, one of its eyes lame from a previous battle.

"Fudge." Wasn't the word her mother used, and it shocked Arleen.

"Mama?" If her mama were dropping f-bombs, Arleen should be scared.

"Stay behind me, fluffykins." The name Mama had given her when she was just a baby and arrived in the world with a full head of hair.

The bear rose on two hind legs, roaring, menacing even while emaciated. It had massive paws, bigger than her head, jagged yellow claws, and a mean attitude.

Mama let out a warning noise.

The bear didn't seem impressed. Judging by the marks on his body, he'd fought for the privilege to stay alive this long. Even if his teeth appeared few and far between, the ones that remained could easily crunch their bones. Arleen bit her lip so she didn't whimper.

Mama muttered, "Take cover, fluffykins."

Hiding sounded like a good idea. Arleen tucked behind a column of ice, so cold she knew better than to touch it—her skin would stick. She waited for her mother to join her. Maybe they could sneak out of the cave using the pillars as cover.

Her mama chose to face off with the bear. Fearless when it came to danger. Mama shifted, her loose clothes accommodating the sudden shift in size and fur. The sleekness of the brown hair had her grimacing at the reminder of her own coloring, more like the bear than her family.

Mama dropped into a fighting stance, shorter than the bear, narrower too. But she was fast.

She dodged the swiping paw. Up. Down. She kicked. None of the blows were hard enough to truly incapacitate, but it caused the bear to stagger back.

Arleen glanced past the bear to see a steaming crevice. Mama had a plan. She would save them.

Her foot slipped, and she staggered. The bear swung at that exact moment, and its giant paw connected. Mama slammed against a pedestal holding a box. It wobbled but didn't fall—the treasure they'd come to see. Arleen really didn't care what was in the box anymore, because Mama slumped and didn't get up, even as the bear charged for her.

"Mama!" Arleen shrieked and bolted from cover, which drew the bear's shaggy regard. It took a step towards Arleen and roared.

Upset, Arleen flipped to her other shape and roared right back.

It wasn't as impressive, and only pissed off the polar bear.

It charged Arleen, and she froze, fear turning her into a statue. She was too small to fight it. Her only option was to outrun it.

She darted for a column, racing behind it, only to scream as the bear rammed it. It cracked, chunks of ice falling from overhead—jagged spears.

Bolting from her column, she moved to another, but the bear followed, ramming its shoulders into the icy support, causing a shower of frozen chunks to rain. It hurt.

Arleen covered her head, running blindly now, panic making her move.

Until there was nothing but a chasm in the floor, no columns. And when she whirled, the bear advanced on her. Slowly. It knew it had her.

She tried to be brave like her mama, a warrior. She faced it with small, hairy fists.

Its mouth opened wide, exhaling humid death. And then...Mama was there! Hands linked so that she might club it. The force of the blow had the bear shaking its head. It reared on hind legs.

Mama expected it and was already leaping and slamming down with her fists. The bear staggered, close to the steaming crevice in the floor. Mama hit again, and again, her face grim with determination.

Arleen began approaching as her mother wound up for a final blow that would topple the polar giant.

Whack. The bear teetered on the edge and lashed out, its reach lengthening past what Arleen would have expected. The claws slashed across her mother's chest. Deep gouges that bled.

Arleen saw the shock on her mother's face. They both missed the second wild swipe from the bear, the one that hooked Mama's ankle. It dragged her off the edge without a single shriek.

Arleen screamed for her as she scrabbled to the edge.

She peeked over. "Mama?" She whisper-cried the word as she stared down. The slit in the earth could have been a few feet or bottomless, she couldn't see far enough to tell. No bear. No mother. Nothing but a rising cloud of steam.

Still, she waited by that crack for hours, looking and listening until she finally realized that Mama was gone. Arleen was alone.

Panic hit her, and she whirled to run, but tears blinded her. In her mad dash, she crashed into the pedestal, her hands not managing to stop her from smacking her face off the box sitting atop it. Her lip split, and her chin dropped hotly onto the stupid thing that'd brought her and her mom here. A special trip for just the two of them.

A nightmare that now had her sobbing and blubbering while bleeding. She grabbed the box, ignoring the electrical jolt and threw it.

It hit the ground and skidded, its passage clearing the swirling mist.

"I hate you!" she yelled. The box had killed her mother.

She stalked over to it and lifted her foot. She would smash it to bits so no one else ever came looking for it.

But as her foot hovered over the box, she hesitated.

The carved wooden square had begun to glow. It lit the unreadable inscriptions on its surface, the keyhole shining the brightest.

Open it.

She pressed a bloody finger to it. She didn't have a key. She wished she did, because according to the legend her mama had told her, the box had magic inside. Maybe the kind that could bring her back.

Arleen grabbed the glowing box and wondered if the lock could be picked. Maybe the fact that it glowed was a good thing?

She hugged it close and wished: *I want Mama.* She wanted to feel loved and protected. To feel safe rather than sad and alone.

Arleen wanted to go back to the carefree happiness she'd enjoyed just that morning. Exhausted, she fell asleep, wrapped around the box.

She woke curled up on the ice, a pretty container in her arms. It would look even nicer on the pedestal.

She placed it atop and then centered it.

My lovely.

My pretty.

It was her duty to protect it, and was the only thing she remembered...

Until the day the people came and broke the curse.

CHAPTER ONE

The ice cracked under Zach's paw, and he leapt before it had a chance to collapse. He really regretted his choice to accept a mission that involved him travelling to the Arctic. The only kind of cold he usually tolerated involved skis and hot cocoa.

Not running for his life, his four legs pounding, trying to outpace the heaving ground caused by the suddenly active volcano. As if the shivering ground and lifting ice chunks weren't bad enough, fissures began hissing with steam.

It meant they had to move fast—*they* being Zach, Nora, and Peter. They weaved past the scalding jets and leapt over chasms that hadn't yet turned into steam cookers. Zach could only hope they made it to their ride before the whole plateau collapsed.

The popping ice began to slow, and they outpaced the destruction as the mist thinned. Zach saw the chopper right where he'd left it on the ice field—military-grade but unmarked. It had special dispensation to fly, and he'd have no trouble, so long as he didn't draw attention.

They bolted for it, legs pumping, bodies low and long. A lion could run up to fifty miles per hour. When this desperate, it was probably closer to sixty.

Once they were close enough, Zach shifted and yanked open the cockpit door. He had to get the engine going. Fast. He'd not been out here long, so it should still be reasonably warm. The engine started, and the blades began turning. He grabbed a duffle bag and opened it before tossing clothes around like confetti. Shirt for you. Pants for me. Unisize rubberized booties. Easier to pack and better than being barefoot when in his two-legged shape. People had a thing about toes showing, especially in cold climates.

A steam whistle popped through the ice as the devastation neared.

Zach barked, "Buckle up, we're leaving!" Without checking to make sure they were secured, he thrust them into the air. Not a moment too soon.

A fissure opened below them, and even rising quickly, the hot gust heated them something fierce. He banked away from it. As they got clear of the steam and into the fresher air, he noticed it. A scent that didn't belong.

But he couldn't worry about that yet. The cataclysm had spread. Cracks appeared ahead of them, hissing steam and forcing him higher and higher. He moved them away, following the coordinates back to the place where he'd borrowed their ride.

With the danger easing, Nora exclaimed, "Holy shit, Zach. I can't believe you came in a chopper."

"Yeah, it wasn't my first choice," he admitted, keeping an eye on his gauges. His first thought when he realized that he'd have to infiltrate the Arctic was actually a snowmobile. A chopper wasn't exactly ideal, given the cold conditions. And they weren't meant for long flights in these types of temperatures. However, given that he didn't know who or what he might be bringing back—or the urgency of the mission—he opted for something a little bigger and faster.

"Glad you found us."

"Only found you by a fluke. I was actually following some of those human mercenaries again." They'd been causing some problems in their desperate attempt to get their hands on a treasure of late. The humans didn't get it, but neither did the good Pride.

"Do you think Svetlana made it out with the box?" Nora asked.

"Maybe. Depends if they got out fast enough." After all, they'd made it.

Peter finally joined the conversation. "Shouldn't we be discussing the fact that the box turned me into a lion?"

"I don't know why you're surprised. The book did, after all, say that might happen."

Peter's voice held wry amusement as he said, "Doesn't mean I believed it would actually happen." He could be excused for the attitude given he'd woken up that morning as a man, and was now a shapeshifting lion. Wouldn't that fuck with some people in the Pride?

"It happened, and now we need to worry about it happening again if Svetlana chooses to use it."

"Use it to do what? Turn people into were—animals? Why?" Peter asked, sounding baffled as to why anyone would choose that.

"Don't you know why?" Nora cajoled. "Admit it, you feel more powerful. You can see better. Hear better. The human you never could have outraced the volcano."

"I won't deny that it feels good."

"Only good?" Nora teased.

"Okay, more," he admitted with a chuckle. "But that kind of magic...there's no way the box can consistently do it. It's got to have some sort of battery or quota."

"What if it doesn't? What if Svetlana and her grandmother did escape, and they begin selling its use?"

"How is more of us a bad thing?" Zach asked.

"The stories show the magic going two ways. What if it can unmake shifters, too?"

An ominous thought that overshadowed Zach's concern over the possible stowaway.

As he flew, Nora explained to Peter what being a shifter meant. The rules. The advantages. The disadvantages. Zach didn't say a word when Nora told Peter he'd have to make a once-a-year vet appointment for his shots and anal gland squeeze.

Not true, but something the older teens liked to tease the younger ones with. A rite of passage for many. Peter was just older than most.

When he began complaining about all the rules, Nora offered to play the world's tiniest violin.

To which Peter laughed and said, "Don't you dare."

Their flirting was both cute and annoying at once. Zach did his best to ignore it as well as the occasional kissing noises. When they started, he focused on the flight and tried to figure out the scent that didn't belong.

Definitely hadn't been there on his trip over. He could only imagine it—*they*—had stowed away in the storage area where he'd tossed some equipment in case things went sideways in the Russian Arctic—which they had, and in spectacular fashion. It turned out two other groups were also looking for the artifact they sought, and in comedic timing, they'd all ended up in the underground cave at the same time.

Which made him wonder. "Who got to the cave first?"

"We did," Nora announced. "Then those bloody humans. Then Svetlana and her grandma."

"You forgot the yeti," Peter muttered.

"The what?" Zach asked.

"When we first arrived in the cave, we encountered a rare Russian yeti. Beautiful creature. Soft with silvery white-gray fur. I called her Fluffy."

"I don't think there is such a thing as Russian yeti."

"Thank you. That's what I told her," Peter exclaimed.

"Then what was it?" Nora huffed.

"Sasquatch," Peter said.

"Isn't that the same thing?" Zach remarked.

"No." Nora sounded firm on that point.

"Pretty sure it and bigfoot are all the same thing."

"Yetis have white fur."

"So do some tigers. They're still in the same family."

The argument kept going, and yet there was a playfulness to it. Nora, Zach's sometimes mission partner, had found her mate.

The hormones rolling off her and Peter were distracting, and rather than have them go at it in the back seat when things got a little too wet and fleshy, Zach interrupted by asking questions about their journey to the cave as they'd gone in different directions—Nora following an old riddle that'd taken her through a hidden tunnel system, Zach following the humans hunting them.

He was never gladder than when he could finally land and dump them off. He hoped he never acted so dumb. The only thing that should ever get such a lovey-dovey stare was blue-cooked steak drizzled with garlic butter. There were only two things Zach loved in life: food and his cat.

The moment they landed, he basically told Nora and Peter to fuck off, but nicely, offering them the use of his rental. He'd hire a taxi to take him to the hotel after he was done with his paperwork. At least, that's what he told them.

As the newly infatuated couple went off, he pretended to check over the chopper, waiting until they were out of sight.

"You can come out now." His curiosity had him sniffing and trying to figure out who'd snuck aboard. He didn't know the scent and wasn't sure what to expect, other than he knew it wasn't Svetlana or her grandmother. Tiger had a distinctive scent. The only thing he could tell with any certainty was that his stowaway wasn't human.

"I know you're in there. Come out." He peered deeper but still saw nothing. Could he be mistaken?

Just when he was about to start rummaging for himself, a rustling preceded the biggest fucking eyes he'd ever seen, a bright and icy blue. Fine features framed by silver and gray hair that hung down over her naked frame.

The petite female—at least compared to him—blinked thick lashes at him, her lip sucked in as if nervous.

"Who the fuck are you?" he barked, not at all taken in by her innocent face.

Only to blink as she replied with an unexpected, "Fluffy."

"Uh. What?" And better yet, what the fuck was she? He took a sniff, then another, because her scent was so strange. Yet...familiar. Hadn't he recently gotten a whiff of it in that cave in Russia where his last mission went sideways—a polite way of saying the wrong side won?

She smelled cold and crisp like the woods in winter with a coppery hint of something else.

Blood.

"You're injured." He reached for her, only to have her bare her teeth and hiss.

"Don't you get snippy with me," he barked. "Show me the wound."

She stared at him cautiously. She didn't understand.

He mimed, pointing to a gash on his arm, then at her. "Are you hurt?"

Her eyes widened, and she nodded. Pushing aside her hair, she showed off more of her nude body and the sluggishly bleeding bullet hole.

Had she been in the cave during the firefight? How had no one seen her?

Unless...

Couldn't be.

He eyed her anew. "Are you the yeti from the cave?"

She cocked her head.

"Guess you can't exactly answer that." Was it even possible? Yetis weren't real. The only Simian-type shifters he knew of were of the gorilla variety, and they preferred warmer climates.

"I'm Zach." He poked himself in the chest.

She smiled. "Fluffy."

Fluffy being the name Nora had bestowed on the beast she'd wanted to adopt as a pet. Wouldn't she be excited to find out that her new pet hadn't died when the cave collapsed?

Wouldn't she be even more surprised to realize that her Yeti was a shapeshifter? Nora wouldn't be able to keep it. They had laws about owning sentient beings.

"What am I going to do with you?" He had no one to foist Fluffy off onto. He'd stupidly sent Nora and Peter off. They were probably cementing their mating bond at this very moment in the back seat of the rental. There went the deposit. But even more horrifying, they were willingly going to bond.

Shudder. The idea of being with one person for life? Never. The only other being he could tolerate for any amount of time was his cat, Nefertiti—Neffi. A demanding Himalayan kitten that had grown into an even more bossy feline. He left her with his father when he had to leave town on business. They hated each other. Which meant she'd be mad when he returned. Would probably piss all over his pillow. Do her nails on the couch. And sleep in her bed instead of with him.

He'd better put in an order with the market now to ensure that he had fresh seafood tidbits to apologize.

Fluffy kept staring at him as if waiting for something.

Oh, yeah. What to do with her? He'd kind of expected her to run off by this point. Wasn't that their modus operandi? Why had she stowed away on his chopper? Given that she was obviously a cold-climate creature, shouldn't she have stayed on the ice fields?

The ice field they may have had a hand in destroying.

Crap.

She'd obviously raced ahead of the destruction and hidden on board, tracing his trail back. On his way in, he'd had to forgo caution for haste so he didn't lose those he was following. The human mercenary team had opted to go in on snowmobiles, easy to follow. When he landed, he was only minutes behind.

"Reckon I can't leave you here." Heavy sigh. "Let's get you somewhere warm where we can get you some food and clothes." He'd seen plenty of nudity in his life, and yet hers distracted him. She had the type of frame he liked, solid if a tad too willowy. Some might have thought her large compared to modern ideals.

Personally, Zach found most women undersized. No one wanted to get a neck cramp trying to kiss someone. Not to mention, fear hurting them, given his size. And what about if he wanted them to do a couple's Spartan race? He needed someone who could keep up. She had decent legs and could probably do a three-legged race with him.

Fluffy was small compared to Zach, but bigger than most of the lionesses and humans he ran into. Over six feet, her frame willowy but strong. Long legs and arms, a short torso with a faint dip at the waist. And her breasts...

Oops. He averted his gaze and pulled off his thick sweater, wishing he'd brought a few more. Explaining why you were outside naked in the cold always caused too many questions. A shifter knew it might have to go native.

Case in point, they'd bolted from the collapsing cavern on four furry legs and raced across the ice field. Human skin would have been damaged by the steam erupting from the rifts. The cold that bit the feet. Which was why he'd ensured that the chopper had a duffle of clothes.

He handed her the shirt. She eyed it and then him. Cocked her head.

"Put it on." He shook it.

She grabbed it and began playing with it, getting it open and jamming it over her head, only to panic once she couldn't find the head hole.

He snatched it free, and she halted in her frantic scramble.

He shook his head. "Have you never worn clothes before?" He would have loved to put the sweater back on. It was freaking cold. "Watch." He showed her how he put it on. Popping his head through the hole.

She studied him intently the entire time. When he handed it over once more, she didn't panic, simply wedged it over her head, offering up the biggest smile.

He must have been tired because he grinned back. "Now, for the arms." He lifted his and then inclined his head.

She managed to get one of them in almost right away, but the other did that thing where it wouldn't let the hand pop out easily. She snarled, and her hand went through the fabric.

She smiled in triumph.

"It's a start. Let's go, Fluffy." He jerked his thumb and started to walk, only to realize that she didn't follow. She hovered inside the chopper, looking lost in his sweater.

"Don't be afraid. Ain't nothing out here. We know the guy who owns this place."

Still, she hesitated.

He took a few steps back, his irritation growing. The urge to snap, "*Move!*," rising to his lips.

She looked scared. Cautious. If she'd never left the frozen plains, then she'd probably never seen civilization.

Wolf girl, meet yeti woman. Why him? This was

the kind of thing better suited to anyone *but* him—someone with compassion and a soft touch.

They needed patience too, of which he never had a supply. So, rather than be gentle and kind, he barked, "Get your ass moving, Fluffy. Let's go. I don't have all fucking night."

CHAPTER TWO

The big man yelled, and she heard her name.
Fluffy.

She'd thought he was leaving her when he walked away, but now, he loomed before her, loud and indicating that she had to move.

She scrambled down onto the oddly flat and smooth rock, the biggest she'd ever seen, extending all around. It provided a place for the whirlybird to land. She'd seen them before. They liked to fly over the ice field every so often, making lots of noise and chasing off her lunch.

She'd never expected that one might save her life. Wounded and scared because of the cracking and steaming rock, she'd exited the cave via a secret passage and stumbled across an intriguingly scented trail. She'd followed it to a dormant whirlybird, and hearing pursuit, hid inside.

She'd almost leaped off when it lifted from the ground, only the quickest peek at the heaving slabs of ice changed her mind. She'd thought herself so clever until Zach confronted her.

He had a name, as did the others with him. She'd listened to them speaking, even heard her name mentioned a few times.

"Zach."

"What?" he snapped, and she understood, even as she had to quicken her stride to follow. He was big. *Very* big. Like a bear, only he wasn't. She'd seen him in the cave. He was a giant cat. She remembered cats, even as she didn't recall ever seeing any.

He had skin that was darker than hers, and only stubble on his head. He had an agile walk, loose-hipped, casual yet alert.

She more or less stumbled along. It had been a long time since she'd worn this shape. A very long time because of the cold. When she went all flesh, she only had stiff fur from previous hunts to wrap her shivers in.

But she wasn't always this way. She used to have a sweater like the one he'd given her. She'd had those things on his legs too, and feet covers. They'd long since fallen to tatters.

He led her to a massive—*building?* The word

hovered, and she gave it meaning as she stared at the square thing with other shapes inset within. He opened a rectangle to show a cave inside.

His lair?

She entered and wrinkled her nose at the smells. He didn't seem to notice and headed for the opposite side. He still spoke, and she found herself understanding a few words.

"...taxi...hotel...doctor."

The last word conjured an image of a male in white, poking her with something sharp.

"Nnoo." The word burst from her.

He paused in his steps and ranting to look at her. "So, you do understand a little."

The sounds had meaning, and at the same time didn't. She rolled her shoulders.

He babbled some more in his language only to huff hotly at the end. "Come."

Since she had nothing better to do, she followed him. He went into a smaller box. There were oddly shaped items in the room, one of them tempting her to sit.

So, she did.

Chair. A thing to seat herself on. Look at her, creating names for objects.

She watched as Zach prowled behind a waist-high object. A desk. He pulled out the desk's tongues and withdrew a box.

Not her box. This one was white with a red, drunken X on it, more like a cross. Opening it, he withdrew some items, and she didn't realize they were for her until he pointed and said, "Show me."

Show him what?

He knelt and reached for the shirt. She slapped at his hand.

He growled.

She growled back.

"I'm trying to check your wound."

She understood *wound*. But didn't know how he planned to help. Would he lick it for her since she couldn't reach?

She lifted her shirt and showed him the sluggishly bleeding hole.

He clucked his tongue as he wiped it.

She hissed.

"Don't be a baby."

She knew *baby* and frowned.

He kept dabbing and peering. "Bullet's still inside."

She glanced at the hole and saw the edge of the object.

In her!

Suddenly panicked, she dug her fingers into the hole, gasped at the pain, but yanked it free, along with the blood dammed behind it.

"Out," she said.

"Well, that's one way to do it," he muttered as he pressed the white cloth to her skin. It quickly turned red. He grabbed another and kept the pressure on. She tried to ignore him.

It wasn't easy. And not just because of his size.

His scent distracted.

His very presence had her lightheaded.

He wound more of the white stuff around her, holding the bigger folded square in place.

Then he moved off and bent over, reappearing with a large box.

"Lost and found. See what they..." Blah. Blah. He spoke, she paid little attention. She was more interested in what he pulled free. More sweaters. Some for the head. Some for the hands. Even one for her legs.

She drew on the garments in the brightest colors she'd ever seen—other than blood, which was always really red. She grinned. "Sweater!"

"Not entirely, but we'll go with it," he muttered.

More guttural sounds that she just absorbed as she put on her sweaters and was finally warm.

"Ah." She sighed.

"Now that we have clothes, I need to call a taxi. Good thing I left my wallet and phone here." He opened a door to another building cave.

Was he leaving her?

She launched herself from the chair, and he froze, meaning her momentum thrust her into him.

He steadied her. "Whoa."

"Zach." She said his name, and his brow creased.

He spoke in those weird sounds that almost had meaning, then heaved a breath. "Fine. You can come."

She stuck close to him as he went into a small cave and rummaged in crevices cleverly hidden.

He held up some small objects that made no sense. A tiny plastic square. Fluttery paper. He stuffed them into his leg sweater, which had convenient pockets built in. She checked her own to find that she had two. She'd keep an eye out for things she could stuff into them.

Maybe the stick in that cup. She grabbed it and gnawed on the end.

It crunched, and something damp shot out.

"Fuck!"

He snatched her juicy stick away. It leaked a dark fluid on him. She licked her lips. The taste wasn't great.

He shook it at her. "No eating pens."

"No." She eyed the shelf with more things. Pointed to another stick that might be tastier.

"No. If you're hungry, have this."

He thrust something that crinkled at her. Yellow with red and black markings.

"Eat." He mimed putting it into his mouth.

She shoved the whole thing in, which wasn't easy. She had to bite halfway and then almost bit her tongue as she squealed.

The sweetness was pure pleasure.

She shoved it all the way into her mouth and chewed. Cooed. Chewed some more. When it was gone, she began looking for another.

Zach held up another of the delicious things.

She lunged, but he held it out of reach.

"M-M-Mine!" She burst for it.

"You can have it in the taxi. Let's go. Come."

She knew *come*. But she wanted her treat now. Leaping off the shelf with the yucky-tasting sticks, she launched herself at his hand and grabbed the yummy thing. Then she shot out the hole to the next cave, then the next. She hesitated for only a second in the massive cavern before choosing a new rectangle set in its wall. She emerged onto more of the flat rock painted with white and yellow lines. But it was the lights bearing down on her with a rumble of a massive monster behind it that had her plastering herself against the wall.

She was still there when Zach emerged. He appeared annoyed to see her. He walked right past to the beast huffing on the smooth rock. He got inside it.

And she had a sudden vision of riding inside one before.

A car.

Zach leaned out and snapped, "Come."

Since she was a long way from her cave, she followed.

CHAPTER THREE

Fluffy touched everything in the back seat. And not just with her hands. He'd known toddlers that licked less stuff.

The cabby kept eyeing her in his rearview, his massive unibrow twitching as if it were about to crawl off his head. The cabby—*"Call me Gerald"*—wouldn't tell anyone about what he saw. The male didn't bear the scent of a shapeshifter, but...something else. Someone who didn't want to be noticed.

"Is your lady friend okay?" Gerald asked in heavily accented English.

"She's from the country." Zach kept it simple.

"Ah." Because that explained everything, even halfway across the world. "Where to?"

Since he had no choice, Zach brought her to his hotel. Nora had a room as well, on a different floor.

An asshole would have interrupted her night of sex and dumped the yeti on her. That same asshole would probably wake the next day, minus his skin. Never get between a lioness and her mate. Right up there with don't touch great aunt Natalie's pecan pie unless she serves it to you on a plate.

A good thing for Nora that he liked her. Not many people could claim that distinction. Nora was good people, though. It should be noted he didn't like Peter. Or Fluffy for that matter. However, he was responsible for her. He'd keep her close until he could hand her off.

Rawr. His inner feline was a little too happy about it.

It's temporary.

Apparently, his lion had other ideas. *Keep.*

She is not a pet, no matter what Nora says.

Then his lion uttered something so shocking and rude that he almost shoved Fluffy out of the car.

Take that back.

But his lion smirked and thought it again. *Mate.*

I don't think so.

Coward.

He was still having his internal argument when they arrived at the hotel, the building old and rundown with remnants of grandeur. It could use a major overhaul. However, you couldn't beat the privacy.

"Ooh." Fluffy had her face pressed to the glass as if it were a fairy tale castle

Zach paid the cabby and then slid out of the back. She kept staring out her side. "Let's go, Fluffy."

"M-kay," she chirped as she hopped out, then took in a deep breath—and gagged.

"Welcome to the smell of civilization, Fluffy. It ain't pretty." He rubbed her back as she took in a ragged breath. When she straightened, her face held repugnance.

He felt sympathy. "You'll get used to it after a while." It became more noticeable when he returned from a place people hadn't really penetrated. He loved those kinds of big, open spaces.

Recovered, she glanced around and then pointed to a streetlight. "Sss-sun." She spoke as if it had been a long time, and her voice still needed a chance to warm up. How long had she been in that cave? Were there others like her?

"Actually, that's a light." He pointed to all the illuminated sources and repeated it until she did.

Her brow knitted as if she were thinking, and she glanced at the ground. Then the street with its traffic.

"City," she stated.

"Yes." Meaning, she did remember and knew some stuff about the modern world. He pegged her age somewhere between early twenties to possibly thirties.

Fit. Seemingly healthy with all her teeth. Only a few scars that he'd seen.

"Did you used to live in a city?"

Her nose scrunched. She understood but struggled to reply.

Before she could get frustrated, he broke in with, "I'm hungry. Let's get something to eat."

Her expression lit, and she smiled as she rubbed her tummy.

Fuck, she was cute, even with her hair a wild mess. He snuck her in the hotel's side door, and they took the stairs up. At this time of night, no one was in the stairwell.

The steps were a thing of wonder for her. She oohed at them and skipped up and down a few times before laughing as she raced them. He had to whistle at the third-floor landing to get her back by his side.

She arrived with flushed cheeks, and part of her bandage hanging loose. He'd fix it in his room. He'd opted to keep her with him rather than book another one. He wasn't sure she could be left alone. Not to mention, given how she stiffened and paused, ready to bolt each time she heard a strange noise, it wouldn't take much to startle her. She couldn't flee under his watch. He needed her secured until he made her someone else's problem.

The door to room 304 opened with a swipe of his

keycard, and she entered, curious but with her shoulders back. She stalked into the room, sniffing, tense but with surprisingly no fear.

She noted the neatly made beds—two of them because Zach liked the choice of mattresses when he stayed places. She ran her fingers over the fabric cover. He flicked a switch, and the light turned on.

He might as well have set off a bomb. Fluffy jumped. Had she been a cat, the claws would have come out. As it was, she went partially furry and hit the floor before scuttling under the bed.

"Fluffy?" Such a stupid name. He really needed to find something more suitable and proper like Melanie or Patricia.

She didn't reply, so he dropped to a knee, lifted the bed skirt, and peeked. He didn't see her, which took him aback. He stood and glanced on the other side of the bed. Nothing. He knelt between them and peeked under the second one. Empty, too.

It made no sense. He glanced once more under the bed he'd seen her disappear under. Just shadows, and yet...he could smell her. As if she were right in front of him.

He reached into a seemingly empty spot, and his fingers encountered an ankle. Despite not seeing her, he grabbed and yanked.

Apparently, not a good idea as Fluffy bellowed,

heaved, and lifted the bed into the air, sending it crashing.

He eyed the disaster, then her. Shook his finger and said, "Bad. Bad, Fluffy."

Rather than appear contrite, she eyed her ankle and then him, arching a brow.

He got the message. "Don't touch?" He nodded. "Fair enough. I won't touch, but you need to listen. No hiding under the bed."

"Bed." She said the word and frowned, then eyed the one she'd wrecked. She indicated it. "Bed."

"Yes. Yours too since you broke it." He moved to the bent frame and lifted it. His turn to arch his eyebrow so she would move. He set the frame down in its spot. It was lopsided, but it would hold the mattress. He threw it on top, then the blankets. The pillows, however, he fired at Fluffy.

The first one hit her, and she exclaimed in surprise, only to realize it didn't hurt. She laughed when the second one smacked her and grinned at him.

A sweet smile that should have warned him. She fired a pillow back, and he caught it. But rather than throwing the second one, she swung it.

He let it connect, then did it right back. Hitting her with the soft plush, her reach better than expected. Faster, too. She clocked him good, and the pillowcase exploded.

Feathers rained down, and her mouth gaped. But in an awed fashion. She laughed as she reached to catch the falling fluff.

He almost joined her. The elation of it filled him still. He'd not had a pillow fight since he was a kid. Seeing the mess, he remembered why his mom had yelled.

"Shit."

"Shit," she echoed.

He startled. "Don't repeat everything that comes out of my mouth."

"Mouth." Her gaze went to it, and his mind tried to go somewhere totally inappropriate. He reined it in.

"Are you calm now?" She didn't seem to be agitated anymore, and the fur had receded.

She glanced from him to the illuminated lamp. "Light?" she asked.

"Yes, light."

"Food?" she said as she looked around.

"Not yet. I need to order up some room service." The Pride he worked for would cover the cost. The menu was beside the phone, translated in four languages. He called in a massive order. A little bit of everything since he had no idea what she liked. What did yetis eat? He'd never imagined they truly existed.

Was she the only one?

And what kind of skills did she have other than lots

of hair and strength? Under that bed, it was as if she'd camouflaged herself to blend in. She'd practically turned invisible, which if it were a species thing, might explain why yetis had not been encountered much— other than the supposed sightings caught on film.

With almost the entire menu ordered and the kitchen staff bribed to deliver it fast, he left her to explore the space, her expression thoughtful as she ran fingers over everything.

Almost everything. She'd not touched him. She'd barely looked at him. He knew because he was hyper-aware of her. Even as he stepped onto the balcony, he kept an eye on her.

He used the privacy to call his boss. Judging by the grumbly, "Hello," he'd woken the Pride's Beta, Hayder. It never occurred to him to check on the time difference. He'd been told, though, to report as soon as he could. He'd sent a brief text while in the air. Now, it was time for the full deets.

"Hey, boss. It's me."

"Took your sweet time calling. I've been waiting since Nora checked in. I fell asleep waiting for you."

"I ran into some unexpected issues." And then because he wasn't one to draw shit out, he added, "I think I found a yeti."

Dead silence.

"Could you repeat that?" Hayder asked.

"You heard me. I have a yeti. Or something like it. In my possession. She stowed away aboard the bird during our escape from the volcano."

"Another yeti?" his boss exclaimed. "Nora was telling me about the one that died in the cave. How many were there out there?"

"Actually, I think it's the same one."

"Where are you now?"

"Hotel."

"You brought a yeti to the hotel!?" Hayder practically shouted.

"Yes, except she's not a yeti anymore. She's a girl. Woman," he amended.

Silence hung again. "You brought a woman to your hotel room?"

"I think the more important thing here is the fact that she's a shifter."

"I disagree on the importance. You brought a woman to your room."

Not something Zach did often, and Hayder would know since they'd roomed together in college. "It has two beds."

"Why not get her an adjoining room?"

"She's a flight risk."

"Look at you, making up excuses to have a sleepover."

"If you met her, you wouldn't even imply that."

"Is she unattractive?"

"No!" A little too hotly said.

"Too young?"

"No, she's in her twenties at the very least. But she's..." Zach sought the right word. "Naïve." He would never take advantage.

"Can she communicate?"

"A little. I think at one time she probably didn't live in a cave, but that would have been a long time ago. She's regressed quite a bit. She'll require some major help."

"The kind of help we can only give here." *Here* being home in the United States. Where would depend on what she needed.

"She also needs a doctor to stitch up a bullet wound. She dug out the slug, and I cleaned it as best I could."

"She dug it out?" Hayder repeated. "Damn. Okay. Um, no words, but I do suggest you find some glue or tape. Because for something this sensitive, I don't know who to call. You're kind of far from home and our usual resources."

"No shit."

"If she heals like us, then just a little something to keep it from tearing open for a few hours should do the trick."

"I'll see what I can scrounge up." A sheet torn into strips and bound tightly should do it.

"Are you sure she's a yeti?" The doubtful query had Zach shrugging even though Hayder couldn't see.

"Maybe? I don't know for sure. She's sure hairy and lanky like one. She walks on two legs. I think she's intelligent, and when shifted, she looks like a silver-haired version of Harry from the Hendersons."

"Of all the weird shit," Hayder muttered. "I'll have to talk to Arik about this." Arik being the Pride king.

"How soon before you can send someone for her?" He wanted her to be someone else's problem.

"I'll have to get back to you on that."

"How long?"

"As long as it takes. This is a bit of a tricky situation."

"Because she might belong to the Russians."

"Partially. But don't forget, she was in that cave with the artifact. The one that changed Peter. She might have been guarding it."

"You think she has answers to its location?" He couldn't help the incredulity.

"No, but she might be able to tell us more about what it can do, or if there's a way to nullify it."

"Fluffy give us a counterspell?" He snorted as he saw her on the floor, sniffing the carpet.

"We don't know what she can tell us. So, for the

moment, that means you stay close and keep her existence quiet."

"Ugh." He didn't hide it.

Hayder chuckled. "It can't be that bad."

Someone knocked at the bedroom door. Fluffy startled and ducked under his intact bed.

He sighed. "I'll keep her out of trouble."

"Not just her. Be on the lookout for more of those human mercenaries. Given their intelligence thus far has been uncannily accurate, she may come to their notice."

"Anyone tries to touch her, I'll handle it." But he had to wonder how many humans the competition would send to their death. Given the number they'd taken out already? Apparently, a never-ending supply.

Zach opened the door and juggled his phone to wheel in the cart of food left outside. The desk already had orders to bill him all expenses with a twenty-five percent tip. He always got excellent service.

His boss wasn't quite done. "We need to find that box, Zach. If you can get her to tell you anything..."

"Yeah, we'll see about that. She's not talking much yet." But he kept seeing hints of confused comprehension. He had a feeling civilization would help her.

"Keep in touch."

"Yup." Zach put his phone away and began moving the trays of food to the table. Once he'd covered the surface, he crouched down, lifted the skirt, and saw shadowed carpeting, replete with dust bunnies. No Fluffy. But once more, he could scent her.

"Stop hiding. I know you're there." When she didn't appear, he growled, a firm sound that had her shimmering into view, meaning the ability to hide in plain sight could be turned on and off.

That was so freaking cool.

She blinked big eyes at him, all innocence and trepidation.

He wasn't about to succumb. "Out from under the bed. Now. And don't you dare wreck it like you ruined yours!" He wagged his finger.

She moved fast enough that she nipped the tip of it before then sliding out the other side.

He blinked. Well, shit. He'd never seen anyone, or anything, move that fast.

Fluffy used that speed to go after the meal just delivered, sniffing a dome before tipping it and diving onto the first thing she saw. The handful of French fries went into her mouth, and her other hand fisted some more.

"You'd better save me some!"

CHAPTER FOUR

Zach joined her, and apparently, expected to share. She didn't want to share. The first thing she grabbed and stuffed into her mouth because it smelled so good tasted even better. Salty. Crunchy.

French fry. Her mind supplied the name. The change in her environment was terrifyingly new and familiar all at once. The more she saw and experienced, the more it was as if her mind unlocked. Things started coming back to her.

Now, if only she could turn off her flight or hide instinct. It coiled inside her, twitching and restless. She was inside a secured space; she shouldn't be so jumpy. Yet she kept diving for cover.

It made Zach so mad. Which was part of the reason she kept those crunchy sticks of goodness away from him. She really wanted them all for herself. They were delicious.

She slapped his hand when he went to grab one. When she wouldn't share, he arched a brow and lifted a metal bowl to reveal a—a—her mind stuttered before blurting—*burger!*

She dove for it, just as he did. She managed to only tear off a piece before he brought it to his mouth.

He took a bite and chewed with extreme relish.

She might have drooled.

He didn't take any pity or share.

She frowned at him and went after more of the dishes. She found a steaming bowl of something that had her gulping and slurping as she tilted it into her mouth, missed it because she leaned it too hard and it slid down her face to drip into her lap.

Only as she finished did she see him staring at her. She wiped her mouth.

He cringed.

She noticed that he wasn't wearing any of his food. He also wiped every so often with the white fabric square he kept in his lap.

Even odder, he ate...slowly. Rather than quickly gulping, he took his time chewing. And chewing. He used his fingers for some of the food, and chose a pronged metal thing for others. As for the liquid in the bowl, he used a rounded thing with a handle. It was curved and held the soup as he lifted it to his mouth and ate it in small sips.

Seemed impractical to her. She lifted the bowl and drained some more. But this time, she didn't let it spill down the sides of her mouth.

When she set it down again, there was no more food, and her tummy started to protest. Not out of hunger, more just plain sensory delight. She ate fish mostly. Red meat depending on what she could hunt. And it was all raw. This, she knew to be cooked. It added a crunchy and tasty aspect to it.

Cooking, a term that conjured up so many images. Cakes. Cookies. Steak. Roast. A torrent of menu choices flooded her brain.

She began to name off what they'd eaten. "Burger. Fries. Soup. Toast." She grabbed a little plastic square and crunched into it, releasing something salty, delicious and creamy. "Peanut butter!" Ambrosia, which she sucked out of the container before going for the next one. Which was jam. She blended the last two and was just finished licking them clean when Zach rose from his chair and headed for the door. She clutched the armrest as he answered and brought in another tray. Her expression brightened.

"More."

This time as he revealed the plates and bowls, he named the foods for her. She recognized pizza and wings. He also had a bowl of green stuff smeared with white cream and crunchy bits.

She enjoyed everything but the leaf. She spat it out. "Ugh."

"It's lettuce."

"Don't like." She reached for more meat.

"Fair enough."

She understood him and froze. Chewed slowly.

He kept talking. "I don't usually eat like this. I'm more of a protein shake, low-carb kind of guy unless I've gone furry. Then I need to eat. Lots."

"Eat." She nodded in agreement. She'd hunted every day, making sure she always had some backup in case she got hungry.

"You need a name."

"Fluffy." Which made her happy. It was a nice word. She knew it. Wanted to hug it.

"No, we can't call you Fluffy. It's demeaning. You must have a name. Jane?"

Her nose wrinkled. That word did not make her happy.

"Sarah? Melanie? Joleene? Betty? Abigail?" He kept naming, and she kept shaking her head.

Finally, she blurted, "Fluffy." Smiled for emphasis.

He sighed. He did that quite a bit.

"Fine. Fluffy for now. But if you change your mind..."

The last of the food gone, he pointed to her. "Let me see your wound. I should have checked it before we ate."

She glanced down. "Boo-boo gone."

"What do you mean, gone?"

She lifted her shirt and showed him how it had begun closing once they got the object out.

"You're healing nicely. Good."

"Good." She agreed. She wasn't happy about being injured. Those bad men had come to her cave and shot off many noisy things.

"You understand me a bit, don't you?"

She rolled her shoulders.

"Do you know about the box and the key?"

Yeah, she knew. She flattened her lips. "Missing."

"Yes, missing."

She'd had one job. She failed. She'd let the box be stolen. "I find."

"You can find?" He tilted his head.

She nodded. Yes, she could locate it. Even now, she felt it tugging at her. Demanding that she protect it.

"Where is it?" he asked.

She stood and twirled until her hand pointed.

"I am not following your pointed finger."

She frowned at him. "Find." Did he not grasp that they only had to go in that direction?

"I need an address, Fluffy. A city name, at the very least."

She didn't understand.

There he went, making that huffing sound again.

He pointed. "Bed. Time for sleep."

Sleep? But she was too excited. Too...everything. "No."

He pursed his lips as if readying to rebuke, and then his expression brightened as if recalling something.

"Do you need to uh, potty?" His gaze dropped to the floor.

Potty? Did he mean squat?

As a matter of fact, she did. She dropped to her haunches, and he yelled, "No."

She held it and eyed him.

"If you gotta potty, use the bathroom." He gestured. Curious, she followed him into a strange, tiny room with a white rock basin filled with water, a stone with strong smells coming from the tiny bottles lined up beside it.

He gestured. "Toilet. Do your potty there." He left and closed the door.

She almost panicked in the tiny space. Grabbed the handle on the door, ready to wrench it open. But then Zach would be upset. Just as he was upset that she'd almost urinated. She didn't understand why. He was the one who asked.

She eyed the depression filled with water.

Toilet.

For some reason, she thought it was meant for sitting to shed bodily waste. Crazy. If she sat, she couldn't see anything coming at her. There were things with sharp teeth in the water.

She squatted over the hole and did her business. Then wished she'd used it to wash herself first.

She sniffed. Her odor would scare her prey away.

"You done?" Zach called from the other side of the door.

Another word she knew. "Done." He came in, saw the yellow water, and then pointed. "Flush."

"Flush."

"Like this," he said as he tugged a lever on the toilet. A loud noise erupted, and her urine disappeared.

Even more amazing, the toilet filled with fresh water.

"Clean." She dove for it, about to splash her face when he grabbed her wrists.

"No toilet water. You wash your hands in the sink." He showed her how to fill the stone basin and empty it. Handed her a small, strange square of fur. A *washcloth* he called it.

He held one of his own and, after wetting it, laved it over his face.

She did the same and felt it refreshing her skin. Scrub, rinse. She did her face and legs. Then pulled off the fabric that kept her warm so she could wash the rest of her.

He stared.

It did things to her body. Especially her nipples and between her legs.

She smiled at him. She knew what this feeling was. The rutting need.

She dropped the cloth.

He kept his gaze on her face. "Keep in mind, nudity is only when you have a place to be private. Those outside this room might not react well if you took off all your clothes."

She understood and didn't. "Body." She glanced at her frame, saw the blood still staining her side, and scrubbed at it.

He stilled her hands. Pulled them away from the pink, puckered skin.

"Holy shit. That healed fast."

She always did unless something was left behind in an attack.

"Let's put you in a T-shirt for bed." He left, and she followed, accepting the fabric he offered, which when on, hung down part of her thigh. It left her legs bare, but it was comfortable. Smelled of him.

"Bedtime," he said, indicating her bed.

It sat at an angle, but she climbed on top, appreciating the softness.

Once more, he uttered a sigh. "Most people use a blanket." He draped fabric over her.

It layered her nicely. She'd not been this warm and dry in forever. The vents in the cave were a wet heat that left shivers and a clammy feeling.

"Fair warning, it's going to get dark, I'm going to turn off the light."

"M'kay." The word spilled from her as she snuggled into the pillow.

Even with her eyes closed, she noticed the lack of illumination. She didn't flinch.

"Zach?" she murmured his name.

"What is it, Fluffs?"

"Good night." The words came to her lips, and there was a pause before he replied.

"Night. Sleep well."

She did, soundly and comfortably. Was in the midst of a dream of a land made of French fries when her rest was rudely interrupted.

CHAPTER FIVE

Zach fully wakened when the door to his room opened. Someone thought to sneak in.

He sprang out of bed, but Fluffy was quicker. She jumped in front of the intruder and turned furry while wearing his *Shaving is for dogs* shirt.

The maid's eyes widened in surprise. She tossed her armful of fresh towels at Fluffy's face. The yeti roared, the kind of sound that promised someone would die.

He bellowed, "Don't eat her." Which, in retrospect, he would have changed.

The maid bolted, and when Fluffy would have chased, he growled. "Don't."

What a start of his day, and before he'd even had a cleansing smoothie. He got out of bed and headed for the statue-like yeti. He could hear the maid in the hall on her walkie-talkie, talking in rapid-fire Russian.

He grabbed Fluffy by the hands, the palms of them softer than he expected. "You can't be a yeti here. Change back. Now."

She stared at him.

"Fuck." Zach scrubbed his face. "We need to leave before she comes back with security." A good thing he was already mostly packed. He threw on a shirt and shoes and glanced at her. Given all the fur, his pants might fit? And he had a hat.

He wasted precious time getting her to put it on. She refused to wear anything but the stretched shirt.

The hall was quiet, still enough to not notice a big, shaggy yeti following him? How much would it cost the Pride to discredit if he was caught on camera?

Hayder would be pissed. He'd told Zach to stay low-key. In his defense. It wasn't even eight a.m. Since when did room service show so early?

Weird. As was the fact that there was no cart in the hall. Perhaps the maid had delivered the towels to the wrong room. Or...someone was looking to flush him.

He stopped a few paces from the stairwell door, and Fluffy bumped into him.

He rocked on his soles. Something didn't feel right. If he were to hypothesize, the maid was a feint to make sure they were there and to draw them out. Inside the room, anyone attacking would have had to come in, one at a time, which he could have handled.

"We need to go back to the room," he said, hearing a creak on the other side of the stairwell door. "Now," he yelled, as it began to open, and gun barrels poked through.

He grabbed Fluffy and bolted, which was when she chose to turn human, long legs flashing as they ran.

"What's happening?" she gasped, her English much improved since last night. A little bit of civilization, and she was starting to remember stuff.

"The maid was a decoy to draw us out."

The elevator dinged and opened on their floor.

More guns. Shit. He dragged her down as they fired. He was less than reassured by the fact that they were darts and not bullets.

Darts meant capture. Death would be better.

Rather than aim for their door, he kicked in the nearest one, not caring if it was occupied. It bounced open, and in one motion, he also pulled his shoe from his foot and whipped it. Clunk.

A shooter went down, his aim totally off, hitting his partner, who forgot about them.

A short reprieve as the farther stair guys got close enough.

Zach shoved Fluffy into the room. "We have to climb." She understood his intent and headed for the balcony, ignoring the people in bed, sitting up and yelling.

"Sorry. Just passing through," he explained as he joined Fluffy outside the sliding glass door.

Third floor. He'd better not fall.

"Hold on to me. I'll get us down." He slipped off his other shoe and flexed.

She eyed him and snorted. The fur emerged, and she clambered down, agile and sure-footed.

He joined her, still as a man, making it to the first floor when he felt the sting.

One dart. No big deal. It was the other five that made him lose his grip and fall.

He awoke...

...in a lap.

A partially naked lap.

He knew that because his cheek rested on a bare thigh. As to who the lap belonged to... The silver hair framing him could only belong to Fluffy. What he didn't know was where they were. He felt a chill, a distinct one. Could hear a rather rumbly hum—of an engine.

Had those guys hunting with tranqs caught them?

He shifted but didn't go far as the curtain of hair parted, and bright eyes peered at him.

"Awake." Fluffy smiled.

"How long was I asleep?" he said, trying to sit up,

ignoring the plaint of his inner feline that wanted to snuggle the bare skin a little longer.

"Long," she replied. "Bad."

They were in the dark, so it took him a moment to adjust and realize their situation.

Look at them, stuck in a cage, the kind with very thick, metal bars. While she wore his T-shirt still, if worse for wear, he appeared to be quite naked. It took only a second to connect the dots. They were in the cargo hold of a plane.

"What the fuck happened?" he exploded.

CHAPTER SIX

What happened was, Fluffy caught Zach when he fell asleep at the worst possible time. Who napped during an attack?

She'd slung him over her shoulders with no idea where to go or what to do. She did something she was good at. She ran. The problem being, she couldn't camouflage with him on her back.

They drew attention, and try as she might, too many eyes watched. She couldn't hide. Oh, how she wanted to. The city was a terrifying place, and a bit of relief filled her when the attackers caught up and shot her with a whole bunch of the sleepytime things. She enjoyed a good nap, really wished she could sleep some more since she'd woken bound hand and foot on pavement. She went a little nuts and bellowed to wake the dead.

Or, in this case, Zach, who emerged from his stupor with a roar, his eyes bloodshot, and his expression crazy. He snapped his bonds when he shifted into his beautiful cat. Despite his earlier admonition about not eating people, he apparently had no problem ignoring that rule.

Which led to more of the humans shooting them full of some more sleepy stuff.

The next time she woke, she was with Zach in a cage. The more they fed her the drug, the less it affected her. He appeared to have recovered faster, too.

He quickly shook off his sleepiness. "Help me out here. Who caught us?"

"Humans."

"They put us in this cage?"

She shrugged. "Sleeping. Didn't see." But their scent was all over it.

"Did those humans say anything to you that you remember?"

She shook her head.

"Was this about the artifact?"

She lifted her shoulders. She had no idea what they wanted.

Zach moved so he could balance on his haunches. He reached out to touch the bars. "No electricity, which is good. Bad news is that this is some heavy-duty shit." He felt the metal and tested its strength.

She could have told him not to bother, but she was going through a bit of a shock. For one, since she'd woken, she'd discovered more and more of her memories had come back.

She knew things. Knew they were in the storage hold of a plane. Knew she was a woman. He was a man. That they were in a cage with a lock.

But she still had no memory of her name or anything else. When it came to life, everything started in that cave. Only she couldn't have said at what age. Sometimes, she remembered herself as a child—scared, and at the same time, endlessly courageous. Then she'd flip from that very young age to now with nothing in between. As if she'd grown overnight.

Who am I? She had a sense of self with nothing to fill it.

Zach had finished his circuit of the cage. It wasn't a long tour.

He crouched in front of her. "We need to get out of this before we land, and they put us back to sleep."

She made a noise.

"Yes, I know that's an obvious plan, but it's something to work with."

"No key." She pointed out the obvious.

"I just need something sharp to pick the lock." But search as he might, he didn't find anything. The only way they'd exit this cage was if someone opened it.

She settled in to wait. It took him a while before he admitted defeat and joined her.

"We'll have to find a way to get someone to open the door. Maybe you can distract them while I take them out."

She snorted.

"What? You want me to distract them while *you* take them out?" He lifted a brow. "Is this because I'm the naked one, 'cause I will remind you, that's my shirt you're wearing."

Her turn to lift an eyebrow.

"Keep it and save the stripping in case my distraction doesn't work."

"Where are we going?" she asked.

The complete sentence took him by surprise. "You got your tongue back."

"Remembering pieces," she admitted.

"Do you remember how you got in that cave?"

"My mother took me so I could see it." The only clear memory she had. Kind of. She couldn't see her mother's face.

"How long ago did she take you?"

She shrugged.

"What happened to your mother?" He clearly assumed tragedy.

He was right. "Bear."

"Oh. Fuck." A sincere thing to say. "Why were you

in the cave with the artifact?"

"Box."

He nodded.

"Protect."

"You're its guardian?"

She nodded. "Find it." The box needed her.

"Find it and do what?" he asked.

She paused because she didn't actually know the answer. It emerged hesitantly. "I guess it would need another hiding spot." But did she want to devote her life to guarding it? No.

She tried to feel sorry about that and couldn't. Even with being caught, she'd already experienced so much. Was starting to remember, too. She didn't have to live in a cave all alone, eating whatever raw meat she hunted. The box was gone. She was free.

Or would be if she wasn't in a cage.

Zach was right. They needed a way out.

The cadence of the plane's engines changed.

"We're starting our descent. Which shape do the kidnappers know you in? Woman or yeti? Because that's the one you should be wearing when they come to get us."

"Both."

"Oh." He rubbed his chin. "All right, then. We'll need to deal with anyone who's seen both your shapes. Once we get free, I'll call it in to the Pride, and someone will send a cleaning crew. Pretty sure the protocol on yetis being outed is the same as lions."

She remembered his feline. "Your coloring is unique." Dark compared to the usual tawny golden.

"I get it from my mother's side."

He still hadn't clued in. "The attackers saw your lion," she pointed out.

"Er...what?"

"The first time you woke, you freaked and roared. It was very loud, and you were furry. You have a big mane."

"Fuck." A word he used quite a bit, despite it being bad. "Guess it doesn't matter now then which they see. They all have to die."

"All of them?"

"Anyone who's seen or heard of us shifting."

She blinked. "That's a lot of people. And isn't killing wrong?

"Depends on how you look at it. Their deaths could save thousands."

"Even if you could, how?" They were stuck.

"I have a plan, but I need your help." He leaned forward as if afraid he might be overheard. "So, listen, that camouflage thing you do? Can you do it on demand? Say, hide well enough that the people offloading us think you're out of the cage?"

Hide in the open? "Maybe. I don't know." All she

knew was that he kept calling her a yeti, but that didn't feel right. *I am...* It eluded her.

She didn't know what or who she was. Yet. But she did know that she trusted Zach, and at least he had a plan.

Only once they heard the machinery for the cargo area did he give her a nod.

Time to hide. She crouched to make herself smaller and then hid. Waited, as did Zach, sitting with his legs crossed, hands on his knees, eyes closed. Appearing nonchalant, even when the machine grabbed hold of the cage and started yanking it. The movement made it hard to hide. Thankfully, nobody came to peek at them until they had been loaded onto a luggage cart.

Since it was night, there were plenty of shadows. But someone still noticed. A very deep voice said, "Where the fuck is the girl?"

Zach lifted his head, smiled, and then said, "I ate her." Then he lunged with a human roar.

The guy shot his dart gun, never realizing that he missed because Zach slumped over and lay still.

The attackers opened the cage so the guy could climb inside for a peek. That was the one Zach tackled as she dove out the door and took care of his partner.

She pounced on him, and they hit the ground hard.

Well, he did anyway. She was on top, adrenalized. And after that long flight, in need of a snack.

Would she get in trouble with Zach if she had a quick bite? The attacker's neck looked succulent.

"No," Zach snapped as he stepped out of the cage, still nude and looking very nice.

"What are you?" blubbered the fellow in English.

Her grumble conveyed hunger.

"No time. Let's go before someone notices."

Zach grabbed her hand, and they ran, with her fur receding until she pounded the ground barefoot, his shirt fluttering around her frame.

As they bolted, a voice spoke up, shrill with alarm. "They're getting away."

"What idiot opened the cage?"

Bang.

The idiot was probably gone.

They ducked around the corner of a building but kept running. They didn't stop until they were in a massive parking lot. A good thing she had a memory of seeing one before, or she might have been a little more awed. Within the ranks, they crouch-ran, him leading the way. She didn't know what he was looking for until he stopped at an older car. The kind with a long back end. He popped the trunk and rummaged, pulling out a bag stuffed with different clothes.

At her questioning look, he said, "Shifters always keep spares in their trunk. This belongs to a wolf, but it will do."

The wolf was built on the smaller side than them both. On her, the clothes were short and tight. On him?

She snickered. The fabric for the top and bottom molded him oddly. The pinkness emphasizing the bold lettering. *Cutie.* Printed on both the ass and the chest.

"Don't you dare laugh," he threatened as they kept moving.

"I think you look great." Better than great, and not just because he was the first person she'd truly connected with in a long while.

He was handsome. And she couldn't help but be aware of him. He didn't know that while he lay in her lap, she'd stroked his hair. Learned his features by touch—another person.

Her skin tingled where they were connected. She loved the feel of his hand laced with hers.

As they threaded through the cars, he stated, "I know where we are."

"How?"

He pointed. "License plates put us in Jersey. Jersey airport, to be exact. Meaning, they smuggled us internationally. The Pride will want to know about this. This kind of live poaching needs to be stopped."

The word *poaching* brought a shiver. "People hunt us." It sounded wrong to say it aloud. She was supposed to be tracking and trapping her prey.

"People have always hunted animals for food or

sport. Getting caught by them is our fault because we know hunting season. We know how to stay safe. The ones we've got to really watch for are those interested in us because we can swap into fur."

"Because we frighten."

"Partially. But there's also a fear that the humans might see us as something they can use."

"So, we hide."

"Yes, we hide. And, lucky for you, I know just the place."

CHAPTER SEVEN

Zach did not warn his dad that he was coming. Time enough, once he arrived, to deal with the old curmudgeon and his complaints. The biggest one being: *Why get a pet if you're not going to take care of it?*

A few times a year, Zach accepted jobs for the Pride that took him away. Yet when he told his dad that he planned to kennel Neffi—the best kitty in the whole damned world—in the nicest place money could rent, his father lost his shit. *"Wasting good money. Might as well flush it. What is wrong with you? I'll take care of it since you can't."*

Given he'd had to leave Neffi for a few weeks at this point, he could just imagine the upcoming lecture.

"Worried?" Fluffy queried, her expression losing

its childlike innocence the more she got away from the cave. She sat beside him in the car he'd borrowed. AKA stole. When he no longer needed it, he'd set it on fire. The Pride would ensure that the owner was completely covered by the insurance company with no rise in premiums.

"Yeah, I'm worried." But not for the reason she likely thought. What would his father say when he showed up with a yeti? What would *he* say? There also existed the possibility that they might be followed. "Those kidnappers came after us pretty brazenly." Would they attack his father's place? Was it even a good idea to go there? He could practically hear his dad barking, "*You think I can't protect myself, boy?*"

"Should have let me eat them." She pouted.

"Are you hungry?" He answered his own question. "Of course, you are. We were drugged, who knows how long ago. With lots of shifting in between." He felt the lack of calories rather intently, too. Another reason to hit his dad's place. Food.

He dug into the console one-handed and found a half-eaten chocolate bar. Who did that? Who took a bite or two and then basically tossed it away? In his house, growing up, they didn't waste. Back then, the Pride wasn't as rich, so families made do with what they had.

"It's partially eaten," he apologized, showing it to her.

Fluffy, not being picky, made it disappear, wrapper and all.

He parked a few blocks away and marked the location. Once he got to his dad's, he'd make a few calls. Could be, instead of torching it, the Pride might choose to take the car joyriding before ditching it somewhere, muddying where it had been.

Getting out of the vehicle, Fluffy followed without being asked, more and more cognizant. He began to wonder how old she was when she got trapped. She certainly didn't act like a child. Would someone develop normally without interaction?

She kept pace and didn't say a word, her gaze instead tracking all around, taking note of the bungalows lining both sides of the street, what some called the post-war homes. Single-family houses erected in tidy rows, creating some of the first suburbias that now, fifty to seventy years later, had turned into a dense city as it grew.

The sidewalk bordered the front yard, a patch he'd mowed growing up with many weeds that shrank as the tree in the front yard grew. Nothing left to mow now. His dad opted for that horrid pebble shit that replaced grass for a maintenance-free space, and the tree was gone. Only a stump remained.

As they went up the short flight of stairs, Fluffy glanced toward the bay window, the blinds not fully closed. She pointed. "Is that a cat?"

A peek inside showed his Neffi—his precious baby—perched on his dad's lap, head pushing into his hand, getting a good rub.

Zach almost slapped himself. It couldn't be true. Except, it was. His cat cheated on him!

Rather than knock and wait for his dad to bellow, he stormed into the house. "Traitors!"

By the time Zach stalked into the living room, his dad sat in his plaid recliner alone, face set in a scowl. "Should have known it was you barging in. Never did manage to take the barn cat out of you. Where's your manners, boy?"

"Don't you dare play innocent. I saw you!" He jabbed a finger at his dad and then Neffi on the opposite side of the room, staring at the wall.

"Saw what?" sniped his father from his chair.

"Drop the act. I know you and my cat have been conspiring against me," Zach accused. His cat had yet to acknowledge his arrival.

"Did you drink too many of those protein shakes? Because you're speaking nonsense," his father blustered.

"Don't deny it. You like my cat." And the most betraying part, his cat seemed to like his dad, too.

His father sliced a hand through the air. "Do not! Disgusting, mangy, filthy thing. As if. I'd prefer a dog over that feline." His father glared. Neffi licked her ass because she cared so much.

"Lies. I am surrounded by lies," Zach exclaimed. "I should leave you both now to each other."

"Want me to kill him?" The soft query had him whirling to see Fluffy eyeballing his dad.

"No killing my father."

"Your father." She perused him. "I see where you get your face."

Wait, what? Was that a good thing? A bad thing? He couldn't tell.

"You brought a woman?" His dad sounded so surprised.

With reason. Zach didn't bring girls over. Actually, he only ever visited with his cat. "This is Fluffy. The Pride wants me to keep an eye on her."

"The Pride left this delicate little thing with a brute like you?" His father, the charmer, stood. A big man, he'd only gotten bigger after the accident left him with a bum leg. "Come in, er...did you say *Fluffy?*"

"Yup. Fluffs, this is my dad, Joseph Lennox."

"Call me Joe," his father rumbled, grabbing her hand and squeezing it. "Pleasure to meet you."

"Hi." She stared at their locked hands. "I'm Fluffy."

"Forgive my presumption, sweet lady, but do you mind me asking what you are? I've never smelled the like. You remind me of the mountains in the winter."

An apt description. "Fluffy is a yeti."

"Er, what?" His dad's startled gaze bobbed between them.

"You heard me. According to Nora, she's a Russian yeti."

"There is no such thing," his dad proclaimed.

"Guess again. I found her in the Russian Arctic."

"And smuggled her home?" His dad added an incredulous note.

"We were kidnapped," Fluffy chirped.

"By who? The tiger mob?" Dad's eyebrows hit his hairline.

"Humans." Fluffy just kept helping.

His father laughed. And laughed.

"Not funny," Zach grumbled. "There's a seriously bad group after Fluffy. Coming here probably put you in danger. We shouldn't have come. Let's go, Fluffs." He turned to her, and his dad predictably blustered.

"You ain't going anywhere."

"I'm serious about the danger."

"You saying I can't handle myself?" His father squinted at him.

He knew his dad could handle himself; it's why

he'd come. "I don't know, old man. Looks like you've been hitting the beer more than the gym."

"I'll have you know it's solid." His father thumped his gut.

As if on cue, Fluff's tummy grumbled.

It drew Dad's attention. "When was the last time this idiot fed you? Never mind. You come with me, baby girl, and we'll get you all set up." Joe hobbled into the kitchen, and Zach knew better than to offer to do any of the cooking. After the accident, his father took offense easily to anything he thought was someone pitying him. It made him extra determined to do everything without help.

Zach would argue more, but the man made a mean grilled cheese and tomato soup.

Basic? Not in his dad's kitchen, given the tomato juice was fresh-pressed and then brought to a quick boil with some fragrant herbs. Sprinkled with mozzarella and served with thick slabs of bread—home-made—buttered and toasted golden with a thick chunk of hard cheddar between the slices. Joe might have retired from the cooking industry, a chef for more than forty years, but he'd not lost any of his skill.

Fluffy started out the meal by shoving a whole quarter of the sandwich into her mouth and grabbing the bowl, lifting it to her lips. Zach just took a bite from his meal and stared at her.

Then he deliberately grabbed a spoon, ate his soup, and sopped his sandwich in it. The bowl went back down, and a determined Fluffy, attempting to mimic, proceeded to make a mess. But she kept trying, while Joe gaped.

Zach ate a single serving and left the rest to her. His dad angled his head, a subtle nudge.

Zach left his stool and went to the pantry, pretending to look for something. His dad closed the door and loudly whispered, "Where did you say you found her?"

"In a cave in the Arctic. I think she'd been living there a while."

"Doing what?"

The artifact part of his mission was secret, even from his dad. Zach shrugged. "Dunno. My job is to keep an eye on her."

"You said people are after her?"

"Yeah. And they don't mess around." The human mercenaries had shown access to resources.

"You need a shower," his dad said, wrinkling his nose.

"We both do." Entering the kitchen again, he caught Fluffs licking the bowl. On the plus side, she didn't appear to be wearing much of it.

She slammed it down and pretended she wasn't eyeing his with the little bit left at the bottom.

"I better make more food," his dad suggested.

"More?" Her expression brightened.

"Yes, more, but only after you bathe. Let's go, Fluffs." He took her down the short hall to the only full bathroom in the house. Pink tile with a bit of white and black. Gold accents. So old, it came back as retro-style.

She saw the toilet and immediately perched on it, forgetting that not only was he in the room, she was also wearing pants. She glanced down at the wet fabric and scrunched her nose.

"You need to pull them down before you sit and go."

"Sit? How will I see the biters coming?" She stared suspiciously at the toilet water.

"Nothing is going to come out of the pipe."

"Wet." Her nose wrinkled as she hopped off the toilet and shoved down the pants. The shirt covered her groin, but still left lots of exposed leg.

He turned his gaze. "You need a shower." He leaned into the shower tub combo and flipped on the water. It emerged in a jet, and she *ooohed*.

"Water." She reached for it and said, "So warm!"

Actually, it was still chilly, but compared to what she was used to...

She hopped in—still wearing her shirt—put her face right into the spray, and sighed. Then squeaked.

"Hot!" She plastered against the back wall, and he

wondered at her reaction until he thought of the volcano.

"Did you sometimes get really hot geysers?"

She nodded. "Bad burns."

"This won't burn you. See?" He put his hand in it. Slowly, she reached for it, too. Smiled.

When she began pulling at her shirt, he knew it was time to go. "Here's some soap. And there's a towel on the counter." He'd pulled one from the shelf.

Despite his inner lion saying he should offer to scrub her back, he left, closing the door behind him.

Sitting in the middle of the hall was his cat.

"Hey, baby. I'm home." He crouched.

Neffi stared.

"Did you miss me?"

Judging by her glare, not even for a second.

"I ordered you some treats."

Rather than appeasing his feline, she glanced at the bathroom door where he could hear splashing and humming.

Neffi uttered a low growl then stalked off, hackles raised.

Jealous. Good. Now, Neffi would know how Zach felt after seeing her with his dad.

He returned to the kitchen. With Fluffs taken care of for the moment, he had time to check in. He borrowed his dad's phone, a cordless digital, and only because they'd phased out rotary. His dad had ranted for months when they made him change out his lime green curly-corded monstrosity. Even the fact that Zach had bought the phone didn't appease.

The voice that picked up his direct line wasn't Hayder's. Nor did it waste time.

"Who is this?"

"Zachary Lennox."

"The same Zachary Lennox who was incommunicado for fifty-five hours?"

He winced. He now knew how long he'd been out for. "I ran into some complications."

"Do you still have the subject?"

"I'm supposed to report to Hayder."

"Hayder is attending the birth of yet another useless boy."

"And you are?"

"Not a biatch you want to piss off," said the biatch. "Has the yeti told you anything yet about the treasure?"

That explained whether or not the lioness on the other end of the line was in the loop.

"Not really. Her communication skills have been somewhat lacking, not to mention our kidnapping had us knocked out."

"What kidnapping?" He related what'd happened

to them and made arrangements for the stolen car to be handled.

"I'll have to let the king know about this."

"Obviously." The kidnappers had to be dealt with.

"Wait until the other biatches hear. We've been bored to death. This will give us something to sharpen our claws for. I've got biatches en route to the airport. Hopefully, we can get our hands on that plane and cage before they sterilize it."

Only the biatches could be excited about animal smugglers who might know their secret.

"Could be they aren't related to the artifact at all."

"Maybe. I mean, I can see why they might want to capture a yeti, though. Either way, someone thinks she's important. Which leads me back to the earlier question. Does she know where it is?"

He thought of Fluffy's random pointing. "She says she can lead me to the box. She definitely wants to find it. She claims to be a guardian of some sort."

"Follow her lead and see if she can locate it."

"Me?" Working alone with Fluffs?

"Yeah, you. We don't have anyone else to spare right now. Or are you trying to tell me your feeble man brain can't handle a job of this magnitude?"

"I'll handle it."

"Good, because I need to be pulling out the old latex suit, not yapping with you."

With that, the biatch on duty hung up, leaving him saddled for who knew how long with Fluffs.

Forever? his inner feline taunted. He might have had a retort if his dad hadn't said, "Why are there bubbles coming from under the bathroom door?"

CHAPTER EIGHT

F luffy was having the time of her life when the
door bounced open. Zach gaped in the frame.

"What did you do?" he exclaimed.

She grinned as she patted the foam expanding all
over. "Bubble bath."

Imagine her surprise when the tub began to fill as
she showered. A hot basin of water that she dropped
into. Pouring a bottle filled with smelly goo, it frothed.
Multiplied. The foam getting bigger and bigger.
Spilling into the small room.

It kept expanding and tickled her nose. She
sneezed, and the bubbles exploded all over. When she
blinked her wet lashes, Zach wore a full white beard.

She giggled as she imagined him in a red suit,
jiggling a round belly.

"Not funny. Water damage is no joke." He reached over and turned off the tap.

Her lips turned down. "Bubbles."

"You have enough bubbles and too much water," he exclaimed as it sloshed over the sides.

He reached into the tub and rooted around.

His face went through a few expressions before settling on disgusted. He withdrew her plug of hair. He gagged as he turned from her, tossed it into the toilet, and flushed.

"You ruined my bath," she complained as the water drained.

"Next time, take a proper one that doesn't cause damage, and you'll enjoy it longer."

"Meanie." She glared.

He didn't seem to care. He held out the towel and looked away. "Let's go, Fluffs."

She stood, and the suds clung to her skin. She stepped into the fabric he held out, and he wrapped it around her, patting her dry. Usually, she shivered by a steam vent until most of the moisture was gone. This was nicer.

"How's your wound?" he asked.

"Gone." She grabbed the towel and showed him.

He went tense and said, "Looking good."

"Am I?" she said softly. She dropped the towel

entirely. Stepped closer to him on impulse. Felt the flutter that happened every time he got near.

"Behave."

"Am I being bad?" She knew on some level she was teasing. Flirting even, as she didn't recall ever doing it before.

"Don't." He grabbed a fresh towel and wrapped it around her. "Not all men will respect you. They might take advantage."

She understood enough to smirk. "Then I'll eat them."

"You're not in the Arctic anymore, Fluffs. You can't just eat the things that annoy you."

"Why?"

"Because you'll go to jail."

The word had her seeing another kind of cage. She shuddered.

"Let's find you some clothes." He led her from the bathroom to a small room featuring a skinny bed atop drawers, a dresser beside it, and posters all over of very athletic men and women. The scent belonged primarily to Zach.

"You live here?" she asked, trailing her fingers over the wood and eyeing the statues on it. *Trophies* was the proper word, and she read his name on each one. Look at that, she could read.

"I don't live here anymore. But I grew up in this house."

"With your parents." Because that was how it worked.

"My dad only. My mom left when I was young."

"Mine left me, too." Her lips turned down. "I don't remember my mom." Only the death. She didn't remember any of her family. Only her purpose. She veered from the sad topic to ask the most pressing question.

"When are we going to find it?"

He glanced at her. "Find what?"

"The special box. We have to find it. Make it safe." The need to secure it beat inside her and roused her anxiety.

His lips pursed. "I don't know where it is."

How could he not feel its pull? She pointed. "That way." The direction tugged at her.

"*That way* isn't enough. You're going to need to be more specific. Can you give me a name? A landmark? Mountain? Or a lake?"

"Mountain!" The syllables evoked a strong image. "A range of them, they're huge, the tops of them touch the sky in places. The valleys are lush and green."

"Sounds like you're describing the Rockies."

It was as if a bell went off inside her. She smiled. "Yes. The Rockies."

"Guess we've got a location, then. I'll book us some plane tickets."

The thing that flew in the air? She shook her head. "No. No planes."

"We wouldn't be travelling with the luggage this time."

"No."

"We could take a train. But that would really cause a delay."

"Train? Choo. Choo." She chuckled as he handed her a clean shirt—his shirt with his scent on it. He also handed her soft pants. Fabric too, for her feet.

"If you want to find that box, then the quicker, the better. Think about it while I clean up your mess."

"I'll help."

For some reason, he looked appalled. "You've done enough for one day. Get dressed. If you can't sleep, find my dad in the kitchen. He'll probably have more food for you."

Food? That had her dressing quickly, even before he left, slamming the door.

She got all the large pieces on and then headed out to find Joe.

The man was in the kitchen, using a stool to spin from stove, to counter, to sink. He cooked.

Her tummy rumbled.

He didn't even look as he said, "Have a seat. I've

got something coming out of the oven you'll want to try."

She fidgeted and was glad when he spoke. Mostly questions that she answered with one or two words.

A restlessness filled her as if she should be moving. The box needed her.

Pulled her.

She took a bite of the hot thing on a plate that Joe slid in front of her. It was beyond delicious.

Between bites of the fresh cinnamon rolls with gooey icing, she told Zach's dad her life story, which didn't currently amount to much. She didn't remember a childhood. And her time in the cave was a blur.

Zach returned and reached for a treat. "Ooh, yummy."

She wanted to slap his hand, but had a stupid thing going on in her head for some reason: *Sharing is caring.* She wasn't sure how depriving herself showed care, but she allowed it.

Then she stared overlong at how he ate the pastry. His lips probably sweet from the sugar, he groaned in pleasure. Having groaned herself, she understood.

She paid attention suddenly to the argument in front of her.

"You should drive," Joe exclaimed.

"Drive where?" Zach asked, licking his fingers

before reaching for a napkin. Was that allowed with these treats?

"Fluffy was telling me about how you need to visit the Rockies to find a treasure."

He glanced at her. "You told him about the box."

Her shoulders lifted. "He asked."

"It's supposed to be a secret."

"It is? No one told me that."

His mouth opened and shut. "Shit. It never occurred to me."

"Not a good secret. You know," she reminded, "Nora. Peter. Hayder." A name she'd heard the first night they met.

"Add a few more," he muttered. "I get it."

"You saying I can't keep a secret, boy?"

"Joe won't tell." Fluffy grinned at him.

Joe beamed. "Already smarter than you, I see."

"What can I say, the apple doesn't fall far from the tree."

His father harrumphed, and Zach smirked. Both stubborn, and yet she felt the bond between them. Strong.

"We can drive to the box?" she asked. When she'd talked with Joe, they'd gone through the various scenarios. Flying scared her. Trains were less than straight forward and tedious.

"By car will take days," Zach remarked.

"Days of you losing whoever might be following," his dad argued.

"I don't know. My car's not good outside the city." Zach shook his head.

"Stupid electric cars. What you going to do when the apocalypse hits and the electronics stop working? Huh?" His dad snorted.

"Borrow your gas-guzzling Impala." The males went at it again.

"Over my dead body," Joe snarled.

"Here's to hoping it slows down the zombies while I make my escape." Zach smirked.

The men stared at each other, and she waited for their next verbal attack. Or would it get physical? She couldn't help but be fascinated, and for some reason, she craved something salty and crunchy to complete her utter enjoyment.

Eventually, Joe relented. "Since it's for a good cause, you can borrow her, but I expect the Monica to come back in pristine condition. No eating inside."

"It's vinyl. You do realize it just wipes off."

"No. Eating," his dad emphasized.

"Fine. No food. I'll pack it with a few things, and we'll get going before four."

"Are you insane? You need a little more time to prep."

"It will take me literally five minutes to put a bag together."

"For you?" his father argued. "Your lady friend needs clothes."

"She's wearing clothes," Zach stated.

"Even foot sweaters," she said, holding out her foot where it dangled loosely.

"She looks ridiculous," Joe hissed.

No, she didn't. She glanced at her bold red shirt with slashes of white with buttons, and her green pants. "I like it."

"See, she likes it," Zach parroted.

Joe shook his head. "Idiot. If Nora or any of the biatches find out you didn't get her stuff, then you'll go missing. When that happens, I am turning your bedroom into an office."

"You don't even own a computer, old man."

"Don't sass me, boy, or I will get the belt."

"You've never owned a belt."

"Because suspenders are a man's best friend." Joe snapped a strap.

"You're always arguing. This is why I moved out. Forget staying here. We're leaving, Fluffy. I'll call the Pride for a ride."

"Leave because you can't handle the truth," Joe hotly declared.

They fought because of her. She put her hand on Zach's arm. He froze.

"Stay. I'll go find the box." He didn't need to help her.

Both men snorted.

"As if you're going alone," Zach stated with a roll of his eyes.

"Your lady friend needs to work on her sense of humor because that wasn't even close to funny. I'll get some food together for you to take."

"And we'll hit the thrift shop and get her outfitted. Happy?"

"Very." Joe smiled.

And she was confused. What happened to their battle?

Suddenly, they were the staunchest allies. She narrowed her gaze. Had they just fooled her?

Zach insisted that she wear shoes. The things for her feet were uncomfortable, a wedge of plastic between her toes, keeping it on her foot. It slapped loudly every time she took a step.

"Good thing it's almost spring," he said as they headed out for the store.

"It's hot," she complained at the bright sky.

"It's thirty degrees Fahrenheit. Hardly."

"Bah," she grumbled, shrugging off the heavy coat he'd told her to wear.

Only because people kept staring did she put it back on and move closer to Zach. In the Arctic, she was an apex predator. But out here, outnumbered with the humans and all their knowledge, she was out of her element.

Entering the store, an impression of too much stuff closing in the space almost sent her running. But then she saw a pretty color.

The pale pink belonged to shoes—pretty ones with a heel and a bow.

She turned to Zach and knew with every ounce of her being, "I need those shoes."

CHAPTER NINE

She said, "I need," and Zach bought her the most impractical shoes ever. A few reasons for that, the top-most being that he couldn't say no to those big eyes.

Damnit.

It didn't help that the heels looked damned good on her feet. Strangest thing, though? She could actually walk in them. She strutted as they headed back for the house, each of them carrying a bag in one hand, the others linked. He could argue that it was so he didn't lose her, but the truth was, he kind of enjoyed it—which he didn't care to analyze. Probably fatigue and residual effects of the drugs. He'd decided to give them the rest of today to fuel up and rest before they took off. He needed to be alert while on the road.

Only it didn't look like he'd get his nap.

As they neared his dad's place, he saw the car

parked across the end of the driveway, blocking the Impala—which his dad had pulled out of the garage and freed of its dust wrap. Dad babied the Monica.

"Something is wrong," he said, driving past without slowing down.

She craned to look behind them. "Joe." With one word, she pinpointed his worry.

"Yeah. Joe." He sighed as he parked the car at the corner. "Stay here?" It came out as a question because he already had a feeling he knew her reply.

She grinned and shook her head. "I can help."

She possibly could. Or she could get shot or taken, and he'd be in trouble. But what about his dad?

"We're just going to check things out. Maybe it's not as bad as we think." The question being: Go in on the sly, or boldly?

"Joe's in danger." And, apparently, that was a big deal to her. She bolted for the door, slamming it open and yelling, "Joe!"

He could go in behind her, or... He ran down the side of the house, vaulted the chain-link fence, and landed within a step of the side door. So old that even when locked, a hard yank would open it.

Except for today. A second too late, he noticed the gleam of new metal.

Dad had changed it?

The new lock clicked, and the door opened, the

muzzle of a gun aimed at his face. The guy holding it had pockmarked skin, his hair cut military-short. "Get inside. We have some questions for you and the woman."

Questions? Sounded better than dying now.

He followed, but upon entering the kitchen, a nasally voice demanded, "Check him for weapons."

A human, notable for his peach fuzz growing in patches, ran his hands over Zach's body. While that happened, Zach took in the situation. Dad sat in a kitchen chair, a gun held to the back of his head, swelling making his left eye shut. His nose showed signs of earlier bleeding.

Fuckers.

His dad had fought. Zach saw the scuff marks on all of the home invaders' bodies. Pockmark, Fuzz, plus two more henchmen he mentally nicknamed Bandanna, and the Fonz.

Fluffs stood by the hall entrance, arms held high given the guy holding a gun on her. She hadn't shifted or done anything crazy. Not yet. But he could see the look in her eyes.

Four humans against three shifters.

He liked those odds, except for the guns. These didn't look loaded with tranquilizers.

"For fuck's sake, Dad. I left you alone for an hour.

'I can handle it,' he said, 'I'm not too old.'" Zach started complaining and caught his father's eye.

"Ungrateful whelp, bringing trouble home all the time. How many times must I clean up your messes?"

"My messes?" Zach didn't have to pretend as this argument was an old and familiar one.

To add to the bizarre argument, Fluffy chose to suddenly shake her shopping bag, suspended from her fist as she announced, "I have tiny undergarments now."

The Fonz muttered something along the lines of, "Nobody wants to see that."

Not true. Zach did.

"Shut it. All of you," Pockmark yelled.

"Or what?" Zach cajoled.

Bandanna was the one to shout, "Or the cat gets it." His foot rattled a lidded bin sitting on the floor. Zach heard an angry yowl.

Someone threatened his baby?

"Don't worry, Neffi. Daddy's here," Zach cooed then glared at the home invaders. "I'm going to give you three seconds to get out before I make your mother wish she'd been on a protein diet and swallowed."

"Do anything, and the cat gets it." Bandanna lifted the lid on the bin and aimed his weapon. *Rowr.* Neffi hissed and swiped.

Fluffy dropped her bag. "Don't hurt the kitty." She shook her finger.

"Tell us where the box is, and we won't," Pockmark said.

"Over there." She pointed right away.

Pockmark glanced as if he could see and then frowned. "There, where? I need a place."

"She can't give you one," Zach interjected.

"Liar. Our boss said you and your little friend know exactly where it's gone."

"Who is your boss?" Zach asked because they'd yet to figure out who was in charge of the never-ending stream of human mercenaries—although these were less professional than expected. More small-time thug.

"Our boss is none of your fucking business. Tell us where it is."

"I don't know."

Whereas Fluffy yelled, "Vancouver."

He glared at her. Was it in Vancouver? The Rockies were close by.

She shrugged as she crossed her arms over her new shirt, printed with the skyline of a west coast city.

"So, you do know where it is." Pockmark shook his gun at them, and Zach was annoyed.

He'd also given them way more than the promised three seconds. "Time's up."

Zach saved Neffi first, tackling Bandanna

around the knees. They hit the floor, hard enough that Bandanna yelped and began rolling, holding himself.

Zach popped to his feet, ducked a wild blow from Fuzz, and snapped a few quick jabs at Fuzz's face until his eyes rolled back.

Bandanna took that time to recover and went to charge Zach, only to scream as he clapped his hands over Bandanna's ears. That took him down for the count.

Turning around, it was to see Pockmark gaping, probably because Dad had gone all lion and slobbered on him.

As for Fluffy, she remained humanish and had her attacker on the floor, pinned by the neck, her calf arching nicely in her new shoes.

Trust his dad to notice and ogle.

In less time than it took for his dad to get some coffee going along with a heated plate of cookies, they had their assailants tied to chairs.

Four of them, and the Pride sending a team to pick them up for questioning.

Fluffs grumbled. "Maybe they wouldn't keep attacking if we chewed on a few on them."

"Send a message. I like it," his dad said, serving the cat some flaky tuna from the fridge.

"People kind of frown on that," Zach reminded.

"Meat is meat. You got no problem buying a steak and eating it," his dad argued.

"Different."

"How?"

"Food doesn't talk," Zach explained, not for the first time.

"Mine sometimes does," Fluffs added to the conversation.

"You know talking fish."

"Is a walrus considered a fish? And I only ate him because he wouldn't leave me alone. Seemed a shame to let him go to waste."

"You ate a walrus shifter?" Walrus as in a big seal-like dude. He rubbed his face. "Nope. Not ready for that."

"How many are the Pride sending?" Joe asked. "Doesn't matter. I better make more coffee." His dad limped off, but Fluffy stayed behind. Neffi chose that moment to show she'd finally noticed his arrival. She arrived to twine around his ankles. He gathered her in his arms and drew her to his chest for a snuggle that had her purring.

"That's my sweet baby." He nuzzled his suddenly very loving cat.

It ended the second Fluffy put her hand on his arm.

Neffi swiped and hissed.

Fluffy hissed right back. With a glare, Neffi dug in her claws and leapt from his arms.

"I promise I'll make this up to you," he hollered after his retreating cat.

"Are you sure it's not food?" she asked.

"We don't eat pets."

"Not my pet." If she'd not grinned, he might not have caught the jest.

"Bad Fluffy." He smiled too, lest she think it a rebuke.

"When do we go?" she asked. She knew the attack had moved up their timeline. They couldn't wait until morning now.

"Just waiting for someone to grab my dad and Neffi." He wasn't about to leave them unprotected. "So, not long." It would depend on how fast a team travelled, or if they could find someone local who might arrive shortly.

"Bad." She glanced at the tied men, none of them dead. Although the guy who got the heel in his throat? He might find talking difficult for a while. Eating, too.

"Yeah. Bad. I didn't expect them to strike that quickly." Almost as if they had somehow known his movements. Impossible, unless...he fired a message off to tech support. *Possibly being followed. Hacked? Going off-grid.*

He destroyed his phone and anyone's ability to

track him. It only took one person to betray, much as he hated to think it.

"I'm sorry," she apologized.

"Don't. It's not your fault. We knew they might come after you. We'll lose them once we hit the road."

"I'm ready," she announced, both her shopping bags in hand.

"I have a box packed in the fridge," his dad said, returning to the kitchen and heading for it.

It was only because he tracked his dad's path that Zach's gaze happened past the kitchen window, just in time to catch the rock as it hit the pane and shattered the glass.

"Son of a gun," his father exclaimed. "Wait until I get my hands on them." His father whirled and headed for the side door, but Zach was still watching and yelled, "Fire!" Because a flaming bottle soared for that open hole.

He reached for his dad and yanked him out of harm's way, shoving Fluffy ahead of him into the hall. He heard rather than saw the whoosh as glass shattered, spreading flaming alcohol.

His father yanked free. "My kitchen!"

Zach turned to see it already engulfed. The men tied to the chairs were its first victims, although he wasn't sure how much they felt given they all foamed at the mouth.

Why was someone so psycho about making sure they couldn't be questioned?

The fire alarm went off, and Zach knew they didn't have much time.

"We have to go, Dad."

"Go?" His father appeared to not comprehend as he stared at the spreading flames.

"It's bug-out time," he said.

The familiar words said often to Zach growing up, wiped the confusion from his father's eyes.

"We better grab the bags." Zach knew better than to argue about snaring the bug-out bag his dad kept in case of the apocalypse. He grabbed the army green camo one from the front hall, along with the gray tone version kept packed for Zach. He noticed a third one in there, bright pink with a sparkly crown. Neffi now had her own.

Fluffy had a tight grip on her bags as she sailed out the door, and his cat followed on her heels.

"Where're the keys?" he asked his father as they raced for the car.

"Here." His father dangled them. "I'm driving."

Zach paused long enough to glare. "Don't you fucking start now. You know I'm trained for this."

"Fine. But don't you scratch her," he warned as he slapped the keys into Zach's hand.

"I'll do my best." Although that would be quickly challenged given the vehicle blocking them in.

They piled into the car, Fluffy and his dad in the back, his baby Neffi in the front. He started the engine, a big rumbly beast. He remembered riding with pride in this car as a boy, knowing he was cruising in style. He'd only rarely driven it.

Smoke billowed from the front door of the house as he reversed, making his dad yell as he drove onto the front lawn and then thumped over the curb, avoiding the car blocking the drive.

Only once they'd left the sirens and smoke behind did he say, "Well, guess there's only one place to take you now, old man."

CHAPTER TEN

The look of horror on Joe's face could only mean something terrible.

"No. I ain't going." Joe shook his head violently.

"You don't get a choice," Zach declared, getting the car onto the highway.

"There's a choice. I'll stay with you."

"You can't come. Who would take care of Neffi? We both know Nonna is likely to make her into a stew."

"Cat stew?" Fluffy couldn't help but sound intrigued.

Zach scolded. "No cat stew. Because my dad is going to make sure my grandmother doesn't use Neffi as an ingredient."

Grandmother. The concept brought to mind an

image of a woman, older than herself, hair graying, lines in her face, but smiling and holding her arms out.

Did she have a grandmother?

"Who's going to protect me from that old bat?" Joe argued.

"She's your mother," was Zach's dry reply.

"A child is supposed to move out, not back in." Joe wasn't about to give in. "And need I remind you? She lives in that seniors' residence."

"It's a two-hundred-acre ranch with guest quarters."

"This is abuse," Joe said, turning to her for sympathy. "He's using this as an excuse to dump me in a home."

She had no idea what to say, but Zach did.

"As if I'd be wasting my hard-earned money."

"You saying I'm not worth it?" his father retorted. As they bickered, she settled into the passenger side of the back seat, trying to process everything that had happened.

The attack. People asking questions of her. Putting her and Zach in danger. His father and now the sassy feline in the front seat.

Also traumatizing? The scuff on her new shoes from when her kick to the attacker's face dragged over his teeth.

She'd need a new pair while she got these ones

fixed. Staring at them, she saw another place, a closet with a three-story rack of them. Heeled. Boots. Open-toe. Closed. So many gorgeous shoes. Did they belong to her mother?

And who was her father? It bothered her that she didn't remember anything. She hadn't been that young when her mother died. Fourteen. Not a baby and yet—

Worry about the box. The terse reminder had her tossing her trepidation aside. Concentrate on the now and the most important thing: getting back the treasure. They were moving in the right direction thus far. It tugged at her, whispering, demanding that she come to it.

And when they were reunited. Then what?

Worry about it later. Sleep.

She slept.

They drove until Zach had to stop for gas. She squatted over the toilet rather than sit, mostly because the visible wet spots were disgusting.

They resumed driving, Zach finally agreeing to let his father take over for the last leg. Since the cat wouldn't move, Zach sat in the back seat beside her and promptly went to sleep. It was easy for her to shift his head to her lap, it reminded her of their time in the cage. A scary yet intimate moment.

She ran her fingers over his temple. Working together, they'd escaped.

He'd proven that she could trust him. He'd keep her safe.

"He likes you," confided Joe.

"No, he doesn't." She understood Zach well enough now to know when she irritated him. Sometimes, she did it on purpose.

"He's never brought a girl home before."

It thrilled even as it saddened. It was probably the last home she'd ever see. Once she found the box, she'd find a new cave to hide in.

Um, what? She heard her voice in her head asking the question, and then got a spooky reply.

You need to guard it. Somewhere remote. Abandoned. She blinked. *No.*

It's your duty. The harshness of it jarred.

Maybe I don't want to guard. She didn't, and yet a part of her did. It pulsed inside her, wanting to get back to the box.

It wasn't normal. Something controlled her.

Sleep.

She woke to find Zach, still lying in her lap, staring at her now. She smiled. He started to smile back, then caught himself and scowled.

He pushed off her lap and leaned between the seats to ask Joe, "Where are we?"

"Almost there." The ominous declaration

happened just as the headlights of his car hit a sign and illuminated it.

Private property. Trespassers will be shot.

Far from friendly, and surely illegal. They saw another sign farther up the road. *Turn back now.* Followed by a, *We mean it.* The winding path took them between trees that pinched the road the farther they went. Watching the shadows stream by, she would have sworn she saw movement.

Light greeted them in the form of illuminated stakes, the kind that charged all day with sunlight and then glowed when it got dark. They outlined a massive gravel driveway that branched off. But they parked by a sprawling building, a place with more than a few additions. The mismatched seams of wood showed where some stopped and started. A massive porch led to the main doors, sporting a half-dozen rocking chairs and two hammocks, one of them occupied. The sleeping person dangled a leg over the side.

They pulled to a stop. "We're here," Joe announced but didn't move. He clutched the steering wheel.

"Why don't you go see if Nonna is up while I get the key to the guest house?" Zach suggested.

Joe flashed him a look. "Why don't you? She's been waiting to see you since Christmas."

Zach grimaced. "I couldn't make it for dinner. She can't still be mad."

"Oh, she's mad," Joe sang.

The argument brewed, and while she wanted to enjoy it, she also smelled something delicious. It had been a while since they'd gotten anything to eat. She spilled out of the car and stretched before yelling, "Hello?"

Zach dove through the same door as her and shh-ed her. "Some of the residents are grumpy when woken."

"Why are they sleeping during the day?" She lifted her face to the dawning morning sun.

"Because that's all old people do is sleep. Which is how I know I'm not ready for a place like this," Joe declared, getting out of the car.

Zach snorted. "You nap all the time in that chair of yours."

"Because of the cat. I can't exactly move while she's having a siesta."

"You are so full of shit, your eyes are brown," Zach declared.

"Doubtful, since I drink a glass of prune juice every day."

Over the noise of them arguing, the oddest sound started and grew louder. A whirring, whistling, then an object flashed by. The shoe caught Joe in the face.

Joe reeled, and Zach laughed. "Looks like Nonna is pissed at you."

Whir. Wing. Whack.

Zach recoiled. "Nonna!" He held a hand to his gut. "Where's the love?"

"What love? You're strangers to me. Ungrateful brats who never visit," a woman declared as she stepped out of the woods. She was short. So very short. With steely gray, coiled hair, and a pink tracksuit that glittered. No shoes.

"You can't blame me for not visiting. You've been gone since Christmas on that cruise. You got back like what? Three days ago?" Joe declared.

"Three days of no love," she argued as she neared.

Neffi chose that moment to exit the car with her tail held high. The moment she saw Nonna, she hissed.

Nonna grinned. "What a good boy, bringing me fresh meat."

"Don't you dare eat my cat!" Zach reached for Neffi, who swiped and drew blood.

"For hurting my grandbaby, I'll make you into mittens, too," Nonna declared.

Joe threw himself in front. "Over my dead body."

"It should be enough to feed the gang for crib night." Nonna eyed him, and Fluffy wondered if she planned to serve him raw or cooked. With his puffy middle, Joe would be crunchy.

"You eat people's faces?" Fluffy asked, her voice low and guttural.

"Whenever I get a chance," Nonna boasted.

Fluffy rubbed her hands together. "Yum. Do you have salt or ketchup?" Her two new favorite things.

Nonna cocked her head. "Who do you want to eat, child?"

"You. Then him." She pointed to the fellow watching from the hammock.

"Fluffy, what did I say about eating people?" Zach admonished.

She pouted. "Nonna said I could."

Nonna snuffled. "Who is this crazy girl? I like her. Come with me. I'll give you something better than an old wrinkly face."

"Bacon?" she asked, following the little old lady's quick pace.

"You like bacon?"

She nodded. "And hamburgers. And fries."

Nonna laughed. "Well then, how about bacon and pancakes, with home fries and juice? Maybe a few eggs. Some toast. You like jam?"

"Yes!" Fluffy followed her stomach and the woman who promised to fill it.

CHAPTER ELEVEN

"I swear that girl would get in the van if you offered her candy," Joe declared, watching Fluffy go off with Nonna.

"She would." No denying that she lacked a certain self-preservation, which made Zach wonder how she'd survived.

"You planning to mate her?"

"What?" Zach halted rather than follow his father up the porch steps. "No. Of course, not."

"I've seen how you eye her," his dad teased.

"I don't know what you're talking about." A lie, because he did. Zach stared at her all the time when he thought she wasn't looking. His father had caught him, and they both knew it wasn't Zach's usual style.

"She'd make a good breeder. Wide hips."

"Dad!" He whisper-yelled his name. "You can't say shit like that. It's wrong."

"Why is it wrong? It's a compliment. She's got some fine hips, made for popping out babies. Pretty face. Little rough around the edges, but then again, so are you."

Zach rubbed a hand over his face. "Dad, I am not making her my mate. She's a job."

"A job?" His dad snorted. "Okay. You keep telling yourself that, boy."

Dad went inside, but Zach paused a moment longer. His dad was wrong. So many levels of wrong. He never intended to settle down. And kids? Other people had kids. He had his cat—who'd followed his father inside.

Was Neffi telling him something, as well?

Still... The thought of it—him and Fluffy?

Nope. And not just because of the species thing. She lacked a maturity he liked in his women. It would be taking advantage of her, and he wasn't that kind of guy.

He entered the compound and headed for the kitchen. While there was a dining area, many of the residents preferred to prepare their own meals.

He knew he'd find Nonna there, and she had a few friends, chipping in to make food, which meant instant rivalry. Who had the tastiest eggs? Scrambled, poached, served with a béarnaise sauce? Bacon, ham, or sausage? Grits and home fries.

So much delicious shit started coming out of that kitchen, but Zach was only allowed a few bites before Nonna grabbed him by the ear and marched him off.

"Can't I eat first?" he complained.

"No. I want to know what you did to that girl. She acts like she's been living in a basement. Eats as if she's never seen food." Nonna peered back at the kitchen where Fluffs went to town, demolishing the pile of food.

He rubbed his earlobe and glared. "She acts like that 'cause I found her in a hidden volcano system in the Arctic."

Nonna blinked a few times. "Found her? And then what? Adopted her like a pet?" She smacked him.

"No, she adopted me. Kind of. She stowed aboard my chopper, so I asked Hayder to send someone. But they told me to protect her, and then we got kidnapped, and Dad's house was set on fire, so we ended up here. Which is probably putting you in danger. We should go."

"Did you just call us weak and old?"

"Never."

"It's a smart thing you showed up here. That child was obviously starving."

"I swear, I fed her. She's a bottomless pit."

"She is rather ravenous. I've never heard of her kind asking for bacon."

"What do you mean, *her kind*? You know what she is?"

"Yes, although it's been a while since I ran into one. They're shy and don't come out of the mountains often."

"Mountains as in the Rockies."

Nonna nodded. "Her people laid claim to them a long time ago."

"How is this the first I've heard of bigfoot being real?"

"First off, that term is derogatory."

"Fine, then. Yeti."

"They prefer Sas'qets."

"Sasquatch."

"That is the more common term, yes."

"They're a myth."

"Because they're good at hiding in plain sight. It's said you can look right at one and never know."

Having seen her camouflage, he understood. "But you knew what she was."

"Only because she's not trying to hide. Her scent is unique when taken out of the woods."

It was. "Where in the Rockies do they live?"

"Everywhere. I'm not aware that they own any one

town or neighborhood. They prefer to blend in and live scattered throughout."

"I wonder if she remembers her home, and that's why she's getting me to drive to them," he mused aloud.

"She doesn't know where her home is?" Nonna asked.

"She lost her memories. Like I said, she might have been missing for a long time."

"Doesn't matter, you should try and return her."

"Assuming she's from the Rockies. I found her in the Russian Arctic."

"Does she speak Russian?"

"I don't think so." He'd never even thought to get someone to ask.

"Even if she's not from the mountains, her kind will know how to connect her to other groups."

"They're shifters like us."

"They don't think so. My understanding is it's because they only exist in a sentient version and it somehow makes them purer of purpose."

"The Sasquatch are snobs?" Could this day get any weirder?

"In a sense, yes. They really don't like to mix outside their own and have made it clear that they're to be left alone. They won't like you holding one of them prisoner."

"She's in danger. I'm protecting her like I was ordered to do." It was a stubborn stance to adopt, and Nonna poked a claw into it.

"Doesn't guarding the Pride take precedence over any mission?"

"I doubt our king is worried about a reclusive tribe living in the mountains."

She patted his cheek. "So dumb. You get that from your mother."

He'd argue, but his mother was dumb. She'd left him behind before he even turned one. Some people shouldn't have kids. Or mates. His dad never did remarry.

After Nonna left to see if the bottomless Fluffy needed more sustenance, his dad took her place, Neffi curled around his neck.

His father cast a worried glance over his shoulder and whispered, "You can't leave me here. There's a dame asking me if I want some custard later on."

"You love custard."

"I think she means sex!" His dad's voice peaked as high as his brows.

Zach had a hard time keeping a straight face. "It's okay to say no, Dad."

"And hurt her feelings?"

"You know, maybe you should see how the ranch suits you as an alternative to city living."

"I'm not moving." His father was stubborn.

"You won't have a choice with your house burned down." He'd seen a message about it on his phone. Total loss. Assumed his dad knew, too.

"I'll stay in a hotel until the insurance pays out and I can get the place fixed."

"It can't be fixed, and you can't live in a hotel for that long."

His dad eyed him. "A good son would take his father in."

"I have a one-bedroom apartment, and I am not sleeping on the couch because you're deluded."

"You're trying to get rid of me."

"No, I'm worried about you being alone in that house, even if it can be fixed." The neighborhood had turned rough since the last recession with houses abandoned as mortgages defaulted. Not to mention, with his bum leg and advancing years, his dad shouldn't be alone all the time. A place like the ranch gave him room and support. Although, maybe he should find a place that wasn't with Nonna.

"That house is paid for. It's mine. It's all I have." His father was stone-cold honest.

Zach's throat tightened. "You have me. And my damned cat. Because, let's both be honest here, she loves you."

His father glanced down at Neffi, twining between

his legs, marking him with her scent. "It started with my lobster mousse. I've never seen someone enjoy it as much as she did. She is the gastric connoisseur I've been looking for. Right, my love?"

Zach scowled. "You stole my cat."

"You stole my youth."

A few more barbs, and then they were hugging.

"You be careful, boy. I might miss you a little if you were gone."

"Barely. I know. Try not to steal anyone else's pets," he said, glancing at his cat, who offered him a nod.

He'd loved her for as long as she would allow it. Now, his sweet princess was moving on.

But so was he. "Fluffy, we gotta get going," he announced, heading back into the kitchen.

Which resulted in him first having to eat a stacked plate of food while Nonna and friends packed a cooler and picnic basket that required both hands to lift.

According to the GPS, they probably had about eighteen or so hours of driving left before they reached the town of Missoula in the lower end of the Rockies.

He did the trip in fifteen hours, with only a few stops for caffeine jolts and pee breaks.

By the time he pulled into a motel parking lot, the kind with fluorescent-colored chairs on the cement patio outside each room and doors painted to match, he would have slept in his car.

Luckily, he got a room, the inside a mashup of brown and beige tones. Brown swirly carpet. Brown comforter with zigzags of dark blue. Textured, cream-colored textured—the easiest to repair.

Two beds, A dresser with a television bolted to it. A bathroom with a half-sized tub and a shower with decent water pressure.

He pointed to it, and sternly told Fluffs, "No water over the edges."

"Too small," she replied with sad-looking lips.

"I need to sleep. Behave," he admonished. He shoved a chair under the door handle to their room for good measure, and then fell into bed, asleep the moment his head hit the pillow.

CHAPTER TWELVE

Zach said to behave.

Which could be interpreted in a few ways.

What he didn't say was to stay inside.

Fluffy eyed the door that he'd blocked. How would she remember anything if she didn't experience and see? Not to mention, the insistent tug had gotten stronger the closer they got to the mountains.

Something had drawn her here. Demanded that she move deeper into the high peaks. The Rockies were beautiful. Tall, and white-capped. She wanted to explore them.

She zoned out as she walked to them, and it took the blare of a horn to realize that she'd somehow gotten outside.

Someone guided her out of the road and exclaimed. "Miss, are you all right?'

"Yeah." Why wouldn't she be?

"Do you need help? Are you hurt?" The man, wearing a T-shirt with a cartoon on it that said, *Have you seen me?* appeared concerned.

"I'm fine. But that's not funny," she said, pointing to the image on his chest. "Our faces look nothing like that."

Leaving him gaping at how wrong he'd gotten his chosen art, she stalked off, gazing in wonder at everything all around.

New and not new. Everything around her was familiar. Had she been to this exact place or somewhere similar?

As Fluffy kept walking, she drew some looks. She'd forgotten her coat again and looked underdressed compared to everyone else. How were they not too hot?

She noticed a pair of women across the street with their coats unzipped. Next time, she'd try that, because no one stared at them. Except for her.

And it drew one of the women's gazes. Her eyes widened. Her lips parted. Her friend stopped talking to her and turned to see what had caught her attention. The friend frowned.

They took a step in her direction.

Nope.

Fluffy decided it was time to slip out of sight. She muddied her trail first. Going up and down streets.

Doubling back. Keeping an eye out for the women. She shouldn't have come outside. Zach would be so mad.

Except when she finally returned to the room, creeping back through the bathroom window, she found him still asleep. Peaceful and warm. She cuddled behind him, wrapping herself gently around his frame, and drowsed, only until he stiffened in her grip.

"Did you break your bed?" he asked tightly.

"Nope."

"Then why are you in mine?"

"Nice," she declared, snuggling him. The scent of him appealed. The feel of him excited.

"This isn't proper."

"Don't care." Rules didn't apply to her.

"I should get up."

"Mm-hmm," she hummed, nuzzling the skin at the back of his neck. He shivered.

"Don't do that."

"Why?" she whispered against his flesh. He trembled again.

"Because."

"*Because* isn't an answer." She sang it as if it were something she'd heard a hundred times before.

"You're an attractive woman who has suffered a traumatic experience. It would be un—"

She stopped him by rolling him onto his back and

perching on top of him, straddling him and offering a smile.

"You're not the one doing anything." *She* was the one craving something from him. She slid down just enough that she could rub against the hard ridge at his groin. "Mmm." Again, she hummed.

He groaned as he grabbed her and flipped her to the side, rolling swiftly out of the bed.

"I can't."

"You suck." The words just spilled.

"Would you feel better if I got you some food?"

"Yes!"

"Why don't you shower while I wrangle some?"

"Okay," she agreed easily. After all, she enjoyed hot water, craved sustenance, and *then* she'd work on Zach for the other thing she needed.

Sex.

CHAPTER THIRTEEN

His lion was pissed that he'd walked away, but what else could Zach do? Hayder didn't tell him to guard Fluffy and seduce her.

She was in his care. He had a position of authority. He couldn't take advantage. But what was he supposed to do if she threw herself at him?

Fight her off?

As she started the shower, he left, locking the door behind him. He didn't worry that she'd panic and bolt anymore. Then again, if she did flee, it would solve one of his problems.

The store across the street sold everything from clothes to groceries and liquor. As well as sex toys hidden behind a curtain that was pointless given the flashing sign that screamed, *Adult Fun.*

He filled a wheeled cart with stuff. Lots of

precooked meat since protein appeared to be Fluffy's preference. He got her a pair of combat boots. Pink-and-grey-patterned with a steel toe. It matched the t-shirt that said, *It's Sasquatch, bitch.*

Returning to the motel, he noted a curtain flicking in the room beside his. Someone waiting for a delivery boy, most likely. Or a hooker. Hopefully, not a noisy one.

Entering the room, he was just in time to catch Fluffy holding a plastic knife to her hair.

He closed the door with his foot. "What are you doing?"

"Cutting it." She tugged at the wet and straggly mess.

"You are not cutting your hair." He loved the sight of it, a shimmery fall of moonlight.

Her lips pursed. "It's all knotted and gnarly."

"Which is why I bought you this." He held out a brush.

Her expression brightened. She snatched it from him and tried to do a long stroke. Then yelled and threw the brush. It hit the wall, hard.

"Take it easy. It's not hard to learn."

"I don't need to learn. I know these things. Brushing my hair and peeing while sitting." She grabbed at her cheeks. "I'm not stupid. I can do so much, and yet I keep forgetting."

"Give yourself time to adjust."

"Why bother?" was her retort followed by a short, bitter laugh. "Once I find the box, I'll be back in another cave, alone again."

"Surely, that's not your only option."

She shrugged. "I don't know. And that's the problem."

"Do you want to guard it?" It had never occurred to him that she may not. But then again, what did he really know about her?

"Yeah-no." It was as if her mouth and mind had two answers.

"How did you start guarding it in the first place?" He retrieved the brush.

"It was after my mom died."

"She told you to do it."

Fluffy frowned. "I...don't remember."

"How old were you?"

"Fourteen."

"Kind of young to be accepting a life-long commitment of that sort, don't you think?"

"I..." She hesitated and ended up saying, "You're right. I would have been too young."

"Meaning, maybe it's time that someone else took on the job." Zach sat on the bed and pointed to the spot between his knees. "Over here. Let me fix that mess on your head."

"Scissors would be quicker," she grumbled, folding to sit on her legs, her heels tucked under her ass.

"As a man with almost no hair, I probably shouldn't say much, but it's fucking gorgeous."

"It's always in the way."

He held a fistful of it and worked at the knots. "If it bothers you, then tie it up."

"With what?"

"I'll get you something." He kept stroking the strands, running the brush through it until she leaned against him, practically purring.

And still, he kept brushing, feeling the silk of it running through his fingers.

When she turned, her eyes heavy-lidded, her lips parted, he tried to remind himself to remain aloof. Professional.

He tried to shut himself off from her allure. She placed her hands on his thighs and leaned forward.

She kissed him. Pressed her mouth against his and didn't move away. A soft touch resulting in an explosion of his senses. Her lips parted against his, caressing him, making him forget.

When he gripped her hair and finally gave in, deepening the kiss, she groaned and straddled his lap.

Which was when someone kicked the door in.

CHAPTER FOURTEEN

She was kissing him, and he kissed her back. Her body was on fire, craving something carnal, only to be interrupted as the door got slammed open. It hit the wall, and someone filled the empty space.

Danger.

Fluffy rose with a snarl, ready to eat the face of whoever had interrupted her. She seriously simmered.

Inside the doorframe, a very tall woman stood, staring at her. About her age and build, but with curly, blond hair, green eyes, and wearing a plaid shirt that seemed familiar.

Before she could blink, Zach blocked her from view. "Who the fuck are you? Get out of my room."

"Get away from her, creep!" the woman warned. "We won't let you hurt her."

"I would never hurt her."

"We heard her cry out."

Fluffy peeked around him to say, "In pleasure."

For some reason, this caused the woman to gape. And the more Fluffy stared at her, the more she felt as if they'd met.

It hit her suddenly. "I saw you this morning. You tried to follow me. It took me hours to lose you."

Of course, Zach focused on the wrong part. "You left the room? I told you to behave."

"Excuse me? You can't order my cousin around, creep," the blonde declared.

"Your cousin?" Zach exclaimed. "You know Fluffy?"

"What the fuck kind of name is Fluffy? It's Arleen, asshole." To which the woman turned to her and said, "Arleen, are you okay? We've been worried sick about you. You've been gone so long."

The name acted as a trigger, a bolt of lightning that exploded her brain with memories.

It started with one that was familiar.

The dream where she and her mom went to the cave with the box. They'd followed some stupid pretend map in a book and ended up there. Laughing and loving the adventure together. Until the bear appeared.

But then the memory expanded, and she saw past

her time living as little more than a savage, almost dying so many times.

The box had found a better guardian. A new bear, the cub of the one who'd died. It set her free.

She was found wandering into town one day, without her mother.

No real memory of what'd happened. Her family was so grateful to have her back. More memories unraveled, spinning and showing her finishing school and graduating, going to college. Getting a job. A life that followed the normal path but never fully satisfied her. She felt pulled elsewhere. Ten years after her return, she decided to go back to the cave as an adult, and was just as easily captured the second time, a puppet to the box. It turned her into a mindless slave. Someone who hunted and ate meat fresh from the kill.

AN ANIMAL.

She gagged.

CHAPTER FIFTEEN

Zach caught Fluffy—er, Arleen—before she fell and held her as she made distressed noises in her unconscious state. He ignored the glaring cousin and her demand.

"Unhand her."

"She's having some kind of a fit. She needs to lie down." He lifted Arleen and lay her on the bed.

The blonde fully entered the room, hissing. "Get your hands off her."

"Would you calm the fuck down? I haven't hurt her. This isn't what you think."

"Did you have your hands on her?"

"Yes. But she put them there." She'd climbed him; he had to hold on to something.

"Liar. You're not Arleen's type."

"Arleen doesn't know she has a type. She's been lost so long, she doesn't remember who she is."

"What are you talking about? She's been gone for six weeks."

"No, that's not right. She said something about being young and losing her mother."

"That would be the first time she went missing. What was supposed to be a sixteen-day trip turned into six months. And she remembered us right away as soon as she came home."

"Only six weeks since she was last heard from?" It didn't seem possible given her state. He had to wonder if the box had something to do with her rapid regression. She'd clearly said she hadn't wanted to guard it. Perhaps it had a protective mechanism that forced living beings to act as protectors.

"Before I keep talking to you, who are you?"

He held out his hand. "Zachary Lennox, East Coast Pride. Currently on a mission for the king."

Her brow rose. "Excuse me. Since when does America have a king?" She blinked as if confused. But her scent... It reminded him too much of Arleen.

"No need to pretend. You know what I am. Just like I'm aware you're a Sasquatch. Arleen is, too."

The cousin's lips pressed tight. "What's a lion doing travelling in our mountains?"

What could he say? What if she wasn't aware of

the artifact? "When Arleen said she remembered something about the mountains, we decided to come here and see if the sight of them sparked anything."

"A likely excuse. Everyone knows your kind are tricky."

"My kind?"

"Cats. All pains in the asses, pissing in the garden. Chasing off the birds."

"I'm a lion, not a tabby."

"One and the same. Her mum won't like that Arleen's taken up with one."

He frowned. "I thought her mother died."

"That was mother June. I'm talking about her other mom, Mama Maureen."

"And you are?" he prodded.

"Klara." She didn't shake his hand, but she did step aside.

The door suddenly slammed open again, and a second woman, followed by a third, entered.

It was if the forest filled the room, crisp and cold. If he'd been in the woods, it would have blended perfectly. But in the city, the Sasquatch couldn't hide their scent as well.

"Get away from her," declared the oldest of the room invaders.

"I'll make you into a rug," said the other.

"Ew. No fur, Pamela," exclaimed Klara. "You know

I can't even stand the fake stuff."

"Sorry." Pamela hung her head, whereas the older woman scowled.

"Both of you be quiet and let me see." The female stepped to the side and peered at Arleen on the bed. Gasped. "I'll be. It is her." A steely gaze turned on him. "What have you done to her?"

"Nothing. She lost her memories. I helped bring her here to see if we could spark them."

Lips pursed. "Her scent is all over you. A cat. Her mother won't be pleased."

"We're not together like that." But had they not been interrupted...

"Hmph. What were your plans for her?"

"I'm supposed to protect her," he admitted.

"Why would she need protection?" the older woman asked.

He wasn't supposed to tell but lying would probably see him dead. At this point, he had to bluff his way out of danger by being bold. "Did she ever tell you about an artifact? From her time when she was missing?"

"Not that stupid box again." The older woman rolled her eyes. "I swear, she truly believed her mother when she claimed it was some magical treasure. Once she returned, she never stopped talking about it and how it had to be protected."

"It's real."

For some reason, that had all three sets of eyes focused on him. "Say that again?" asked the oldest.

"I said, the artifact exists. And she was guarding it. Only a bunch of people showed up at once, a fight broke out, she got shot—" At their collective hissed breath, he worried for his safety, so he kept going. "But she escaped before the volcano exploded, stowing away aboard my chopper."

"You fly choppers?" Pamela fluffed her hair.

"Yeah. Anyhow, she didn't know who she was, and when I called it in, they said I should give her a hand. And that was a good thing since the people who went after that box came after her next."

"Why?" Klara blurted.

"I won't protect it!" The words erupted from Arleen, and she jerked on the bed before sitting upright. She opened her eyes and saw him. Her gaze lost its panic and softened. She sighed his name. "Zach." And then reached to touch his face.

"What is going on, Arleen?" the older female snapped.

Arleen bolted out of his lap and froze, eyes wide. Her hands twitched by her sides before she waved and managed a weak, "Aunt Francine. Klara. Pamela. Fancy seeing you here."

CHAPTER SIXTEEN

The memories slammed into her.

Who she was.

Why she'd gone.

What happened.

And now, to pay the price.

Aunt Francine looked livid. "You went looking for that box? After what it did to your mother?"

It should be noted that Aunt Francine often looked angry. She also didn't often leave the compound. But when her cousins had spotted her that morning, they must have called her. This was about to get ugly.

Fluffy, who was baptized as Arleen Bethany Smith, winced. "I was just trying to deal with my past like my therapist told me to."

"Dealing with it means being responsible. It's calling us, letting us know how you are, *where* you are.

Giving us an itinerary, phone numbers. Because then when you go missing, we don't have to worry that you're dead. We've been searching for you. Your poor mum is worried sick." Francine didn't ease up.

Every word of it was true. Arleen had lied when she left because she knew to expect a tirade from her mom. An overprotective mother in her youth, after the first time she'd gone missing, Mum had locked her down tight. She didn't even like it when teenage Arleen went to the store on her bike to get a treat. That was where Aunt Francine had stepped in. She'd gotten her mother to ease up. And by *easing up* it meant she could drive into the city if she had a valid reason to go, but she couldn't be a minute late getting home, or it was meltdown city.

Stifling didn't even begin to describe it.

Aunt Francine took a breath and went to go off again, but Zach stepped in.

"Give Arleen a break. She obviously didn't mean to get fucked over."

"Because she didn't listen," spat her aunt.

The underside of the bed called to Arleen. She wanted to hide. Avoid this conversation. This place. "I didn't do it on purpose to get lost. Stuff kind of happened."

"Happened because you lied! You told your mum you were going on a museum tour of Italy. When you disappeared, we wasted all that time looking in the wrong place."

Arleen fidgeted. "You know I couldn't tell. I knew she'd freak out."

"With good reason. You went back to the place that killed your mom and almost took you. Do you have any idea of the nightmare you revived when you stopped answering? You broke her."

Ouch. Her shoulders drooped. Always with the guilt. Because Arleen had almost died, she had to be Bubble Wrapped for life.

Was it any wonder she escaped?

"Leave her alone, she wanted closure." Zach came to her rescue.

"Closure isn't going back to the place that destroyed both of her mothers."

"I'm an adult now. I needed to face my fears." Needed to find that stupid box. The one controlling her. The one calling to her, even now.

"Adult, and yet dumb as a rock." Francine shook her head.

Funny how this conversation reminded her of Zach and his dad.

"Let's go. No point in delaying it." Aunt Francine stood by the door and waited, a guard waiting for a prisoner.

On the one hand, she could go after a box that

would turn her into some mindless protector, living like an animal and alone until she died. Through door number two she'd have to face the music in the form of her mother losing her shit. There would be tears and yelling, threats, and blanketing guilt.

Her shoulders hunched more.

Zach cleared his throat. "She doesn't have to go if she doesn't want to."

He said it aloud, and there was a moment of stunned silence before Klara laughed, then Pamela, the sound low and mean. Not the greatest cousins. She'd been happier before they moved in with Francine.

"You have done enough. Run back to your king. We'll handle things from here on out," Klara said with a sneer.

"I'm not going anywhere until I complete my mission."

"Hard to complete if you don't have permission to be in our territory."

"Are you coming out and claiming it? Because word has it, the wolves already think they own it, and their Alpha is actually aiding in our search for the artifact," he drawled.

When had that happened? Had he been talking to his Pride the entire time?

She felt out of the loop. Reeling still from everything that had happened.

Perhaps her mother was right. She should never leave home. But then she wouldn't have met Zach. She glanced at him.

He faced off against Francine as if he'd do battle. For the box or for Arleen?

Help him find it.

The voice in her head decided for her. "I'm coming. Just give me a few minutes to talk with Zach. Alone."

"About?" her aunt asked, brow arched. "What could you possibly have to say to *him?*" The inflection went well with the disparaging look she cast at Zach.

The man who rarely smiled, offered a half one that wasn't amused at all. "What she has to say is no one's business but mine."

Did he think it was about the box, or what'd happened? She didn't know which she preferred.

"It's our business because she's family." Cousin Klara tsked, butting in. "Not that you can tell. Always been selfish." This from the girl who liked to borrow Arleen's new clothes and return them with stains or tugs on a thread in the fabric. Oops, how did that happen? But the one time Arleen had borrowed a shirt and Klara thought it looked faded after, she'd had to give her money to shut her up about it.

"Yeah," piped in Pamela, whose last original thought had come before the hundredth bottle of peroxide. How she even still had hair was a testament to the follicular genetics in their family.

Arleen was lucky. She didn't have to mow often when in her less furry shape because her fine tendrils were so light they were almost invisible.

"Whatever you have to say can be said in front of us." Aunt Francine folded her arms. Klara mimicked her.

Arleen bit her lip. Telling him about the box wasn't the issue, it was saying goodbye. Something about Zach appealed and still drew her, even with her memories back.

Especially with, actually, because she recognized the rarity of her attraction to him.

No one had ever made her heart race like he did. But did she really want to be the loser who admitted it out loud to the hot guy? Would she be a coward rather than try? He'd not really done anything to show his interest. On the contrary, he was super grumpy most of the time. Kept telling her that they couldn't. Yet...she couldn't help but have a feeling.

But admitting it in front of her aunt and cousins?

"I need to talk to Zach about the box," Arleen declared. Did she see a hint of disappointment on his face?

"Always with that stupid box. Send him an email. We're leaving."

"Then you can go without me." Her turn to cross her arms.

"As if we're letting you out of our sight!" Aunt Francine declared with a narrow-eyed gaze.

"I can handle myself."

"Apparently, not."

Arleen's lips pursed. "Might I remind you that I've survived one of the harshest environments on Earth with basically nothing, facing off against polars and the Russian yetis? Twice."

"Wait, there really are Russian yetis?" Zach asked. However, no one answered him because a three against one war was on.

"By the looks of it, you had to be saved by a man," Klara cajoled.

"At least I can find a man," Arleen retorted.

"Do you even know what to do with one?" Klara countered.

Francine took offense. "Watch your language."

"Sorry." Klara wasn't apologetic. She was vicious. "For a girl who couldn't supposedly remember her family, how did you end up here?"

"Not because I wanted to. The box is close by," Arleen muttered. She could feel it calling to her from somewhere in these mountains. Probably in a new cave, waiting for her to join it until she got old and another came to take her place.

Zach turned more serious than usual and asked Aunt Francine, "I don't suppose you've heard any reports of any tigers around? A young woman and a much older one."

"Tigers?" Pamela's expression brightened. "I always wanted one of those."

"No tigers," Francine decreed. "And no more stalling. Let's go, Arleen."

Arleen glanced at Zach. He said nothing. Her cousins and aunt looked expectantly at her. To them, the answer seemed obvious. She'd go home with them and accept the verbal punishment coming her way.

But that wasn't the only reason she dreaded leaving.

She cast Zach a panicked look, but his expression, scowl-free for once, revealed nothing.

"I can't go. Zach needs me to find the box." She used him as an excuse.

And for once, he tried to be understanding—the jerk. "If you need to be with your family, go. I'll figure something out."

"You can't find the box without me." Nor did she want anyone else to find it. It belonged to her.

"Maybe that's for the best, given what it's already cost you."

"At least one of them is smart," muttered her aunt.

"What if I don't want to go?" She couldn't help

but huff angrily. She really didn't. Because she already felt stifled. Depressed. Why couldn't she be free?

"You're a Sas'qet. You belong with us." That kind of declaration by her aunt didn't help.

"You don't own me." Why did her family have to feel like a cage?

"You owe it to your mother," Aunt Francine rebuked.

Arleen shook her head. "Owe her what? An apology? Then what? She'll make me promise to never leave, and while I don't want to, I'm going to break that promise. You know I'm not like the rest of you." A Sas'qet was supposed to be the happiest in the mountains. Mostly solitary, hiding from civilization.

But Arleen had always wanted to roam.

Francine stared at her. "I am well aware of your penchant for wandering, but your mother isn't like other people. She needs you."

If only her love didn't suck everything from her. "I'll come talk to her, but I'm not staying."

"We'll figure something out."

The biggest concession she was going to get from Francine. "Let me grab my things."

Francine glanced at her watch. "You've got fifteen minutes. And only because I gotta run over to the store and buy a few things. I promised your mum some yarn she refuses to buy online because they want to charge her shipping."

Aunt Francine left with Arleen's protesting cousins in tow.

"Sorry about that." She felt a need to apologize. Look at the mess she'd drawn him into.

"Don't apologize. I can see why you'd want to forget. Reminds me of Dad and me."

"Except your dad genuinely loves you."

"Your family does, too."

"In a twisted way." She sighed. "I don't know how I didn't remember."

"The artifact. Apparently, it has more than one trick."

She grimaced. "I don't want to guard it anymore."

"Then don't."

"Easy to say. Even now, it calls to me." She hugged herself and looked at the north wall.

"Where?" he asked.

She pointed.

"Not very helpful," he growled. "Still no location?"

She shook her head but had an idea. "Pull up a map on your phone."

"I don't have one."

"How do you not have a phone?"

"Do you? I ditched it because I thought someone was using it to follow us."

"Good thinking since we do seem to get caught a lot."

He almost grinned, then ducked his head. "Oddly enough, I'll miss you, Fluffs."

"I don't have to go." She could stay with him. He just had to say the word.

"Despite the fighting, you should go home. Let your mom get over her panic. Rest. Heal. Forget the box. Forget everything that happened."

Everything? What if she didn't want to forget him, though? What if she wanted more than just a kiss to remember?

Getting her memories back meant knowing that what he made her feel was unique. Not the desire. That was quick and cheap. He...ignited her.

He'd also saved her.

Teased her.

Helped her, even though he didn't have to. And she still had about ten minutes before her aunt came to get her.

She kissed him and felt his shock at the press of her lips on his. She kissed him hard as she shoved him into the wall. He hit it and went still. Frozen. She almost stopped.

But then, as if something within him broke, he began to kiss her back, his mouth hard and insistent against hers, his hands cupping her ass.

Their tongues meshed, hot and wet. His fingers slid past the elastic of her pants. She gripped him. No finesse to her pushing down his trousers. They had no time for languorous exploration.

This was their last chance.

It made them both frantic.

She hooked a leg around his hip, and his hands under her ass gave her the extra height she needed to sheathe him inside her.

She gasped as he filled her. Thick. Hard. He pulsed into her and buried his face in the crook of her neck, sucking the skin.

He whirled so that her back was against the wall and lifted, giving him a better angle to penetrate. He thrust into her. Deeply. Satisfyingly. She clung to his shoulders as he pressed, grinding the tip of himself in a way that had her gasping and squeezing for more.

Over and over, he pumped. Thrust. He gave it to her, and she took it. Welcomed it. And when he would have kept his pace measured and slow, she growled. "Harder. Faster."

He shuddered, and she cried out as he let go of his passion.

It didn't take long for her to come. And he roared as he joined her.

He held her after their shivers subsided, and she could have stayed like that forever, but the clock was ticking. She didn't want to smell like sex all the way home. If she did, she'd never hear the end of it. She threw herself into the bathroom and did a quick clean and coverup.

As she emerged, she heard a knock and a brisk, "Time's up. Let's roll."

His eyes hooded, Zach leaned against the dresser, pants only partially zipped. "Guess you'd better get going."

"Yeah. Can you let me know if you find it?"

"Sure."

It was awkward. Especially since he wouldn't look at her. He stared at the wall as if he couldn't bear one last glimpse.

Whereas she couldn't help but soak him in.

Bang. Bang. Bang. "Come on, Arleen."

She gave him one more chance to say something. To ask her to stay.

When he remained silent, she left. And she didn't look back.

CHAPTER SEVENTEEN

B y the time Zach whirled to say he'd changed his mind and ask her to stay, the door slammed shut.

He sagged onto the bed. Spent. Not just his balls but also his emotions.

His lion was pissed.

The man was sad.

So, when his door got kicked open again, someone almost got their face eaten until he recognized the three biatches looming.

"Lacey, Lenora, and Lana?" Elite Pride Operatives. And he only knew them by name because he'd actually done a few missions with them. It left its mark. They were terrifying. He felt especially bad for their nephew, Lawrence.

"Where's the yeti?" Lana demanded.

"Gone. She left just minutes ago with her family."

"Fuck," Lana, the potty mouth of the group, declared.

Lenora waved a hand. "Doesn't matter. Probably better this way."

"Better how?" Because it sure didn't feel better to Zach.

"Because now your mission can shift focus from babysitting to retrieval of the box."

"I was already look—"

Lana sliced a hand through the air. "We don't have time for you to pretend you actually have a voice. We're here. We're in charge. What we do know? The artifact is somewhere in these mountains. Svetlana and her grandmother were last spotted in Jasper, Canada."

"It's here?" He arched a brow. Maybe Arleen really *could* sense the box. He'd begun to wonder once he realized she had roots in the area.

"It is, and we can't let it fall into the wrong hands."

"Isn't it already?" From what he knew, Svetlana and her grandmother didn't seem like the most trustworthy custodians.

"Are you being smart?" Lana lasered him with a glare.

"No, ma'am. What do you need me to do?"

"Follow your girlfriend."

"What? I don't have a girlfriend."

Lenore snorted. "Oh, please. Her scent is all over you. Can't believe you let her leave."

"I had no choice. Her family made it pretty difficult." Beyond difficult. He'd thought his dad a master manipulator of emotions, but Francine was a level more diabolical.

"Surprised you let her go, given she's still being hunted."

"Are you sure? How?"

"It doesn't matter how. Lucky for you, we took out a team preparing to capture you both. But they'll send more."

The threat to Arleen and her family was how and why he found himself surveilling the Smith compound, a sprawling multi-hundred-acre property surrounded by protected federal land. Awesome, and at the same time, impossible to protect. It was just too vast.

But he and the Elite Pride Operatives—code name The Aunts—took out the small teams of humans that kept coming, trying to capture a live one. Never more than five. Every single one died, but they did have one thing in common.

A tattoo on their bodies. The same thing. A key.

The Pride's research team seemed convinced that they'd somehow stumbled across an order dedicated to the artifact's recovery. Where had they come from? No one yet knew. It was as if they didn't exist. No finger-prints. No facial match. No DNA. Nothing.

Nothing but an endless supply, none ever big enough to truly make a dent in the defense.

In the week he'd been watching, they'd taken out three attacks. But there was no sign of the missing tiger duo or the box. They had groups scattered throughout the Rockies, waiting for Svetlana to surface. A young woman travelling with an old, ornery Russian dame would stick out. Or so you'd think.

What no one could explain was why Svetlana had come to the Rockies. Where was she headed? Why?

He wanted to talk to Arleen about it, only to realize that he didn't have her number. The closest he got to her was when she stepped outside during his watch. She didn't tend to go far, just to the edge of the culti-vated yard, leaning on a faded log fence rail. She'd stay there until someone emerged from the house, yelling her name.

Most likely her mum, given they sometimes fought before heading inside.

Every day, Arleen emerged more and more often, her misery plain to see. Why didn't she leave? Did she need rescuing? Should he step in?

A few times, she turned from the north and stared right at him. Or so it seemed.

His lion urged him to go to her. To claim her.

What if she didn't want to be claimed? She'd just gotten her life back. Not to mention, how would her family react? Because he already knew he couldn't stay. He would take her away, and not just because he couldn't live in the house with her family. He wanted to bring Arleen places that made her smile.

Talk to her?

Don't talk to her?

Indecision plagued him until he got the call, and Lana said, "They've located the tigers."

CHAPTER EIGHTEEN

A week of being in her childhood home only exacerbated the urge to leave. Every day, Arleen had to fight from jumping that fence and running until she found Zach or the box, depending on her mood.

She knew he was out there. Watching. He and some other lions. Her family had spotted them the moment they started spying. But Zach never tried to get close enough to talk. Could be the thing she felt between them wasn't as real as she'd thought.

She'd been looking for that missing something in her life for a while now. Went to Russia thinking her past held the solution to what was lacking. She found the answer. It just wasn't what she expected.

She wanted love.

Companionship.

Excitement.

Knowing Zach was out there, protecting, comforted her. It made her imagine the impossible.

Her family thought it was hilarious. "As if we can't handle ourselves," Klara kept declaring.

"I wish they'd stop pissing on all the fence posts," her mum grumbled.

Pamela pouted. "The lions are ruining all our fun." She enjoyed hunting for sport, not food.

To which Aunt Francine replied, "Better they get caught killing humans than us."

Killing. Humans. They were still coming after Arleen because of the box. A box that neared, which helped her not run screaming down the driveway.

Life fell back into a familiar routine with her mum being tragic, and Aunt Francine—not really her aunt but the name kind of adopted after she became her mum's lover—trying to appease Mum by making all kinds of romantic gestures. Klara was a bitch. Pamela was a dumb bitch. Everyone screamed and fought. It never stopped.

Every time Arleen walked outside, Mum lost her shit. How long before she was allowed to go into town?

Arleen tried to remind herself that Mum did it out of love. After all, the last time, Arleen spent years talking about the day when she'd go looking for the box. Her mum had dragged her to a therapist for countless sessions before Arleen realized that she should keep the box feelings to herself.

Took more than a decade before she finally caved to the urge and went searching for it.

In a sense, Mum was right. Her obsession had almost killed her. But it also let her meet the one man who made her want to abandon the compound even more than a cursed box did.

She missed Zach. His scowls. His growl. His body. His presence.

"Are you moping again?" Pamela complained, joining her outside. "That's all you do."

"What would you prefer? That I sleep until noon and repaint my nails daily?" she snapped.

"You really should do something about those," Klara joined in to gang up on her.

"My nails are fine." Slightly rounded and kept short.

"How long before you run away again?" Klara asked.

"Why?"

"So I can book my next vacation. Between your mum and mine, it was a fucking nightmare when you disappeared."

"I didn't do it on purpose."

"Well, maybe you should," Klara declared.

"Meaning what?"

"Even I know what she means," Pamela stated with a roll of her eyes. "Stop hiding what you're doing. Just tell her when you're going and where."

"She'll tell me not to go."

"Go. And then a text to say you arrived alive. A text each day to say you're there and where there is."

"It won't work." Arleen shook her head.

"You've never tried. You always lie to her and make it worse."

Arleen wanted to deny it, only to realize that Klara might have a point. When she'd scored tickets to go see a concert, she knew her mum would say no. So, Arleen had told Mum she was going to the theatre and then getting ice cream. Only her mom decided to go see the same movie, didn't find her there, and then turned the town upside down looking for her.

"Why are you trying to help me?" Because since her cousins had arrived in her life, it had been nonstop snark as they tried to adjust to a blended family that was like oil and water.

"Because your mum is crazy, but we still like her." Klara shrugged. "And when she's not losing her shit over you, she can be lots of fun."

"If you like making jam or playing Scrabble." Her nose wrinkled.

"Which we do," Klara stated.

"Speak for yourself. My favorite game is still

Tourist." Pamela never tired of it. The game involved showing themselves discreetly to humans camping in the mountains without getting caught on camera or in person. There was much arguing still about the video of a silhouette caught in 2007. They all agreed it was real, but no one would take the blame for having been photographed.

"Aren't we too old for that?" Arleen reminded.

"You are so boring."

Arleen would take boring over the things she recalled having to do to stay alive. She'd never take anything for granted, especially the ability to buy food at the store.

Her cousins wandered off, leaving her to think about the suggestion of not hiding her movements from Mum nor asking for permission. Just do it. And keep doing it. Could it work?

She lifted her face to the sun and had her eyes shut when she heard a vehicle arrive. It had no sooner parked than she tingled.

Could it be?

She whirled to see Zach getting out of the car.

"Zach?" She smiled upon seeing him and ran, only to slow at the sight of his face.

For a moment, his lips curved in reply, only to turn down again. "Don't look so happy."

"Why not?"

"Because I have shit news. Svetlana and the box are possibly headed this way."

The very idea gave her a chill. "Here?"

"Maybe. She was recently spotted about two hours out. Someone on Twitter posted a picture of her sharing a burger with a tiger."

"But why come here? She has the box."

"No idea. But this is our chance to destroy it."

"Destroy it?" The idea filled her with equal parts relief and horror.

"Yeah. Seems the king and your grand poo-bah chatted about it and don't think it's the kind of thing we should have around."

Destroying it would end the curse.

"Let's go." If it was coming for her, she wanted it to be far away from her family.

"Go where?" Mum snarled.

Annoyance filled Arleen as the air shimmered, and out of nowhere, too many family members appeared. Not just Mum and Francine. There was uncle Frank and his wife. More cousins, blood relations this time. An army watching the compound and now taking too much interest in Zach.

They stared at him, but none more intently than her mum.

Standing closest, with her brilliant red mane only slightly gray with age held in a braid, she looked ready to wrestle. "Leave." She might be short at only six feet, but Mum had a voice that carried.

Zach didn't bend. "I will go when I'm done talking to Arleen."

"You mean done filling her head with nonsense about the damned box," her mum sneered. "You aren't taking my daughter anywhere."

"I'd say that's her choice to make, ma'am." Zach sounded cool and confident.

The *oooh* came from everyone watching.

Her mum arched a brow. "We all know she doesn't make good choices. She almost died. Again."

"But didn't. I'll bet she does a lot of things that she could almost die doing but doesn't. Like crossing the road."

Mum's lips pressed tight. "She's not safe out there."

"Not all danger is physical. Some of the things that hurt most are done with the best intentions," was his soft reply.

Mum reeled.

Arleen felt sorry, but not enough to say anything.

"She's staying here." Mum wouldn't back down.

Neither would Zach. "Only if Fluffs says she wants to."

"I'm going with him," she said. Never mind he didn't show up with a declaration of love, she couldn't stay.

Mum went furry in seconds and roared. She lunged for Zach.

Having seen what those hands could do to coconuts, Arleen threw herself in front of him. "Don't you dare touch him."

"I will dare." The words might be guttural, but she understood.

"No, you won't. You can't keep me in a prison forever."

"This is your home."

"Not for me, it isn't. Not anymore. I have to go."

"What if you don't come back?"

She grabbed her mum's hands. "I'll always come back. And I'll be good about calling and texting. You know what they say about the bird and the cage?"

"Keep it locked?" Pamela offered.

"Set it free." Mum's lips trembled. "But—but—"

Aunt Francine barked. "For God's sake, Maureen. Let the girl go. You're stifling her. And frankly, I'm tired of hearing it."

"Don't tell me how to parent," Mum screamed back.

Once more, Pamela showed her annoying side. "If she goes, can I have her room?"

Whereas Klara raised her hand. "I'll take her clothes."

"Don't touch my room. Or my stuff," Arleen declared.

"Quiet!" Zach bellowed. Being the loudest voice, it quieted the chattering. And little Asmodeus, a young boy, sitting on their mother's hip, eyed him with sudden hero worship. "You all heard Arleen. Respect her wishes."

"Don't talk to me about respect, lecher. I know you seduced my baby!" Mum wagged a finger.

"Actually, Mum," Arleen admitted with some pride, "I was the one who seduced *him*."

"Nice!" exclaimed Klara, only to get glared at by Francine.

"She can't just leave. She hasn't packed." Mum tossed out a few tacks in the road to delay her departure.

Zach snorted. "I know about her bottomless stomach. I've got food in the back."

"Ah, isn't that sweet?" Klara sighed.

Pamela gagged. "I smell meat."

"Well, duh," he muttered. "We all know Fluffs is a carnivore."

She leaned close. "They're vegan."

"But you're not."

"Not since my first trip to the cave. Although, I prefer my meat cooked." Remembering herself scarfing it raw made her sick now.

As Mum consoled herself in Francine's arms, little Asmodeus mused aloud, "I've always wanted a cat. Is Arleen gonna keep it? Can I pet it?"

"Maybe when we get back," Arleen promised. She grabbed Zach's arm and glanced at his face. Hard and grumpy as he faced off against her family, but when his gaze met hers, she saw the softening.

Just for her.

She smiled. His lips did something that took the sting out of his sharp, "Are you done reminiscing about the good ol' days with your family, Fluffs? We've got a job to finish."

Was the box the only reason he'd come?

CHAPTER NINETEEN

Zach wanted to expose the lie he'd just uttered. He'd not come here because of the stupid box but because it gave him an excuse. A reason to be close to Arleen. He'd missed her. Missed the way she smiled at him, like when he arrived—beaming from ear to ear because she was genuinely happy to see him.

Her mum wasn't. She wailed as they left, saying that he was stealing her baby while threatening bodily harm against him. It didn't help that her cousin, Klara, asked if they needed condoms. Pamela said she was getting paint chips, and her aunt... Francine rolled her eyes and indicated that they should go.

As they drove away, Arleen remained quiet. Too quiet.

"So, how are you doing?"

"I feel like the worst child in the world breaking my mother's heart," she admitted.

"Is she always like that?"

"To a certain extent. It got worse after my other mom died, and I was lost. I guess me going missing again put her over the edge."

"Must have been hard for you."

"No worse than what you experience with your dad, I imagine."

"I only have my dad riding my ass. Looks like you have a choir."

Her lips twisted. "They do often seem to work against me. But mostly, it's because I don't fit in. I don't want to live quietly in the mountains."

"Doesn't sound like you want to go back after we find the box."

"Dunno. Depends."

"On what?"

She slanted a look at him. "Actually, who."

"Oh."

"Is that all you're going to say?" Her voice turned tight, and it occurred to him that she was anxious. Worried.

"Shit, I am handling this all wrong." He swerved to the side of the road, hard enough that the car skidded on the gravel shoulder. "Actually, there's a lot I want to say. Such as, I am glad you came with me because I don't think your family would have appreciated me carrying you out."

"My mom would have torn your arms from your body and beaten you with them if you tried."

"Yeah, well, I would have still done it. Because I missed you."

"Missed me so much you didn't call? Text? Visit?"

"Don't have your number, and I wanted to."

"So, what stopped you?"

He glanced over. "I wanted you to be sure you were actually interested in me. I didn't want you mistaking gratitude for actual affection."

"How gentlemanly of you."

"Not really." She'd not been around to see how surly he'd become.

"And when you made that choice for me, when did you ask me what I wanted?"

He stared at her. "What do you want?"

"What if I said you?"

He dragged her close for a kiss.

Had she frozen, he would have stopped and apologized.

Had she made any sign of dissent, he would have gotten out of that car and walked to civilization, never to bother her again. But she kissed him back.

Grabbed his face and kissed him so hard, their teeth clashed.

There was some huffing and cursing as they undid seatbelts and he shoved his seat back as far as it could go.

Not really far enough.

He pushed open his door and slid over the hood of the car to the other side. She'd just unbuckled and swung her legs out when he dropped to his knees. The gravel bit into his flesh, but he didn't care.

He tugged at her pants, with her lifting her hips just enough that he could slip them off. Her panties were no obstacle. He shoved those aside and buried his mouth against her.

She was hot. Wet. Quivering with the first lick. She had a foot on the dash, the other over his shoulder. She was jammed against the center console, panting as he licked her, spreading her nether lips to flick her clit. He worked her until she cried out and came against his mouth.

And still he laved her until she was raggedly panting again, mewling at the pleasure. Only then did he undo his pants and kneel once more, cupping her lower body to bring her against him.

He sank into her. Over and over. Sliding into her heat. He felt her tightening around him, but the angle was horrible. He couldn't find a rhythm.

He lifted her from the car and sat her on the hood, getting the traction he wanted to plow deeply. He thrust as she held on to him and kissed her as she came again. Still kissing her when she bit his lip hard enough to draw blood. His body jolted. He exhaled her name as he spilled into her.

Then he simply held her.

Held her and hoped it wasn't the last time he got to feel this bliss with her. But the future was uncertain, and not just because of the tiger that suddenly stood in the middle of the road.

CHAPTER TWENTY

Most people would have reacted to seeing a tiger where a tiger didn't belong. However, Arleen focused on the more important thing that had been hammering at her all day, something she'd been trying to ignore.

The box was here. Literally. Walking out of the woods in the hands of the one who'd stolen it.

Zach zipped his pants as he whirled to confront the threat, placing his body between Arleen and the box.

She wasn't ready to deal with it. Would there ever be a good time?

And then she got anxious. He wanted to take it from her, wanted to destroy it. She had to stop him.

Arleen shoved at Zach and hopped off the hood. Her long sweater covered her to mid-thigh, but she remained barelegged and uncaring as she walked to the woman who'd stopped in the middle of the road. She had blond hair drawn back from a gaunt face showing exhaustion, but her eyes were steely with determination. She held out a knapsack and, even without opening it, Arleen could tell the box was nestled inside.

"Take it." The woman, who had to be Svetlana—who else would travel with a tiger?—shook it in her direction. "Take the cursed box."

Yes. Take it and hide it. In a cave. Far, far away from people.

"No." She said it aloud and in her mind. "No. I don't want it." She backed away.

Svetlana's mouth rounded. "You have to take it. The box told me you would."

"It lied."

"No." Svetlana shook her head. "You can't say no. I won't keep it. The whispers. Always in my head. Talking. Threatening. It's trying to change me. I won't let it." Svetlana screwed her eyes shut and clenched her fists.

She'd managed to fight the box thus far, better than Arleen had. But it wouldn't be long, the cracks were there. If Arleen did nothing, Svetlana would have no choice. She'd be the new guardian.

For a second, jealousy filled her at the thought, at someone else getting to keep it. And then she remembered that taking the box meant giving up Zach. A life. Happiness.

Protecting it wasn't worth that price, and if the box wasn't happy about it, then maybe it should have been more reasonable with its demands.

Rather than wait for a reply, Svetlana dropped the knapsack on the ground and whirled to walk away.

"You can't just leave it there!" Arleen exclaimed.

Svetlana kept walking, heading for the woods, the tiger trotting by her side.

Zach knelt beside the knapsack but didn't touch it. He tossed her a look. "I say we run it over a few times before we bring it in to the experts."

As Zach rose and headed for the car, a shot rang out. He hissed in pain, grabbing his shoulder. "Down," he yelled, which wasn't the best advice.

Ducking would leave Arleen in the open. A round whistled past her cheek. The next hit Svetlana, who yelped as she hit the ground. The tiger lost its mind and roared as it charged the five guys spreading out from the woods. All men dressed in identical combat gear.

How had they found them? Did it matter? She knew what they were after.

The box. And even if she didn't want it, she knew they couldn't have it.

Arleen dove for the damned thing and bundled it

under one arm, ignoring its pleased voice. She wasn't doing it for the box. She shifted as she ran and heard cries of surprise. "It has the artifact. Shoot it! Shoot the bigfoot."

Her feet weren't big. A respectable and buyable eleven in a family that averaged thirteens for the women, and customized sizes for the men.

Arleen loped into the woods, a forest that she knew like the back of her hand. With a mother who home-schooled—because god forbid Arleen be out of sight—she'd had hours, days, weeks, *years* to learn every single crevice. After her first return, roaming their land was the one thing her mother allowed. However, she did take to following her, which led to her staying close to home.

The knowledge of her current location guided her feet, but she didn't go too fast. She didn't want to lose her pursuers because she had a plan. Every so often, she halted to let the humans catch up, hiding within yards of them, and then purposely showing herself to have them running after her again.

The forest turned to stone as she hit the edge of a rocky precipice. The gorge dropped about a hundred feet into a river with violent rapids. The current traveled hard for a few miles before spilling over a small waterfall into a lake. She knew its route well. Not being allowed to go to amusement parks, she'd created her version of fun.

With the knapsack in hand, she waited. Soon, they arrived, all five humans, their attention focused on her and the dangling bag.

Four of them aimed weapons, while the fifth held out his hand. "Give us the box."

She shifted, glad that her sweater had survived the transition if baggier than before. "Why should I? Who are you?"

"Give us the box." The leader waggled his fingers impatiently but didn't answer her second question.

"And if I do?"

"We go away."

Would they? And what would they do with the box? They'd shown themselves as having no regard for life. Imagine the evil they could accomplish with it.

"I don't think anyone should have this kind of power." She slapped the knapsack onto the rock. She did it again and again while he shouted. "Stop!"

Because she couldn't be sure slapping it was enough, she stomped on it. Rammed her foot onto the bag until it became obviously flat. She then kicked it over the edge.

The leader's expression went blank. Then cold. "Kill her."

CHAPTER TWENTY-ONE

The injury slowed Zach down, but not enough for him to ignore Fluffs being chased by bad guys.

He shredded his clothes in his haste to go after them, the wound in his left shoulder, meaning he did more of a three-legged run to keep the pressure off it. The good news? The bullet went right through. The bad? He didn't have time to stop and apply pressure.

Following the trail proved easy, the humans weren't trying to mask their pursuit. Even odder, Fluffs didn't seem to be concealing her route. He knew how well she could hide, so why did she deliberately leave traces?

When the tree line ended, he saw the backs of the humans, all of them facing someone standing at the edge of a cliff.

He was in time to see Arleen jump.

"No!" It came out as *Rawr!* And led to the humans jerking to see him.

Not exactly a great idea as the guns lifted to take aim. Bad odds, but he couldn't exactly run away.

Sometimes, it hurt to be a hero.

He ran for the most scared-looking one, who squeaked and jerked his gun, which led to the guy beside him yelling, "Hey, watch that thing." As they all had their attention drawn, Zach twisted, winced as his shoulder protested, and pounced on a third, who really should have been paying attention.

Four and five tried to shoot, but like a certain military group in white armor, their aim proved atrocious. Not many people learned to shoot moving targets. It was harder than they imagined.

Guy number three panicked and ran, tripping over his feet, and the gunshot proved loud and final. The stupid and clumsy shouldn't own weapons.

The guy under Zach was out, and as he rose to three legs, he felt more than saw the weapon being trained on him. He whirled, expecting to get shot, only to see a branch swung by a very annoyed Svetlana. She knocked the guy out, and the tiger took down the other human.

With the enemy under control, he headed for the edge of the cliff and glanced over, hoping to see Arleen holding on. The rock had no spots to dangle, and the water below looked cold. It moved rapidly, meaning his gaze went upriver. And then he saw her, a silvery head bobbing amidst the dark and angry blue.

It was going to be cold, but he jumped. He hit the glacial water, and his balls climbed up into his throat. It was that fucking cold, but easier than expected to stay with his head above water. He let his body follow the current, using his paws to push off the rocks as he swept past them.

He couldn't see Arleen ahead of him and had to hope that he'd hear or see her before tumbling past too far if she had gone ashore.

A distant roar made his balls climb a little higher. Of course, there would be a waterfall.

Over the edge he went, suspended in mid-air for a moment with a view of a gorgeous valley. Big lake. Bigger forest.

Then he dropped and hit the water. Sank but never touched bottom. He kicked to the surface, following the light. He burst from the water and swapped out of his freezing fur to yell, "Fuck, that's cold."

"Out here, it's what we call refreshing."

He heard Arleen's voice, yelling over the spatter of the falls. He trod water, turning until he saw her, sitting on a rock in the sun, wringing out her sweater.

A gentleman would have looked away from her body.

As her love, he had a right to ogle. She smiled when she caught him. "You jumped."

"I did."

"How did you know it wasn't dangerous?"

"Didn't care. I wasn't letting you go alone and have all the fun."

"Don't know if I'd call that fun. It used to hurt less when I was younger." She stretched and winced.

He laughed. "We're not that old. But I agree, let's not do that again soon." He dragged himself onto the rock, no clothes to worry about meant the sun did its best to warm his sac out of hiding.

"You're hurt. I should go back and eat those humans' faces." She growled as she tore a strip from her sweater and did her best to bind his wound. The water had washed it clean, but while sore, he was more interested in her.

"Are you okay?" he asked, the nearness of her intoxicating his senses.

"Yes."

"What happened to the box? Did you lose it in the river?"

Her expression turned triumphant. "I smashed it before I dumped it. It's gone now. I'm free."

"Good. Because I don't want to lose you." He dragged her close and kissed her.

"I'm never getting lost again."

He nuzzled her. "How far to civilization?"

"Far. But if we wait, they'll come get us."

"How long do we have, do you think?"

She smirked. "How long do you need?"

Not long, as it turned out. Their kisses turned frantic right away. Their hands stroked and squeezed. He sat on the rock, and she straddled him, taking him deep. The muscles of her channel fisted him, and he buried his mouth against her neck. Feeling her pulse. Not just under her skin but within him, as well.

Forever. His mate.

"I'm glad I found you," she said, snuggling close afterwards, the sun warm on their skin.

"Me, too, Fluffy. Me, too."

EPILOGUE

Later that afternoon, they awoke to an audience.

It started with a not-so-whispered, "I don't think they used condoms."

Followed by Maureen saying, "I knew she'd be fine."

Which led to much groaning. He finally opened an eye to see Arleen's family crowded around them.

But the absolute cherry on top? Too short to be seen in the back but definitely heard? His dad and Nonna.

"Why in all the hells is he lying naked outside in the middle of the day? Must be nice not to have to work."

"Work should be balanced with nature." Maureen was closest and hopefully not homicidal to find her daughter in his arms. Someone offered him a robe. Not his first choice, but it covered the nudity well enough.

The situation didn't please Nonna. "You better have mated that girl and not taken advantage. I won't be congratulating you on any bastard babies." Nonna was old-fashioned.

"Any babies they have will be loved no matter what," was Maureen's huffy declaration.

"Too much love, and you smother them," Nonna declared.

As they faced off, Arleen snuggled her face into his chest. "Can we run away?"

"Yes."

"Far away?"

"Oh, hell yes."

Although, first, they had to do a stint at the condo because the king wanted to make sure that even though the box was gone, no one would be coming after them.

To everyone's relief, the attacks stopped.

The key tattoo on the human attackers never resulted in anything concrete.

And Zach found out that Arleen was the best lion's mate a man could ask for. Except when she ate the last rack of ribs.

"That was mine!"

She held it on her fork and smiled. "Wanna wrestle for it?"

"Actually, I'll trade you something for it." He pulled out the box with the ring, the one he'd had made with a pretty pebble he'd bled on when he stepped on it during their rescue by the lake. He'd later found it tucked into his robe pocket and thought it an omen. He had it set on a band. He dangled the ring. "Want it?"

Her gaze hit it and froze. Her lips curved, but she was looking right at him when she said, "Mine."

MONTHS LATER...

Joe brought Nefertiti—Neffi to her subjects—to visit Zach, her previous servant. A decent human. He'd been good at feeding her quality meats and respecting her boundaries. Gave great scratches.

But he left town often. And the last time, he returned with a female.

As if Nefertiti would share.

Zach's father made a good replacement. He'd learned how to scratch behind her ears and provide his body as a heated cushion for her ultra-important naps. But he didn't worship her like Zach used to. Why, he expected her to eat out of a bowl. She'd yet to train him better.

It had been a while since she'd last seen Zach. In

that time, he'd managed to impregnate his female. She had good hips, it would be an easy birth.

Nefertiti had been quite happy to lose that ability. When she woke in that awful-smelling place, she was more perturbed by the spot they'd shaved on her belly. However, now, she didn't need to worry that her dalliances would result in litters that would suck at her tight teats.

Joe set down her carrier and unzipped the door. She stepped out and was gratified to hear her former servant exclaim, "Neffi! Gorgeous girl, come say hello."

As if she'd abase herself. Bad enough she'd come to his wretched place in the city with way too many lions. Pretentious creatures thought they ruled the world.

Let them pretend while she really made a difference. While her servants reunited, she went exploring. Saw a scrap of lace hanging and knew it must have been left for her. Tugging with a claw pulled out a drawer from the dresser. It was filled with all kinds of soft fabric. A bed for her!

She turned in circles, digging her claws into the material, tugging loose threads, shredding the lace, getting the pile just right when her eye caught on an interesting glint. A glance into the mirror across from her showed the object sat above her. On the dresser.

Did she really want to exert herself?

With a grace her servants envied, she moved from the drawer to the dresser top and stalked over to the ring. The one Zach's human usually wore on her finger. But the female had been gaining weight. She'd removed the ring and left it out.

Nefertiti poked it. It wobbled in reply.

How dare it threaten?

She pounced at her enemy and tumbled with it. The ring fled and teetered on the edge, trying to jump. She batted it into another direction. It headed for another edge.

Oh no, it didn't.

Nefertiti soared and hit the ring with her front paws and sank her teeth into it. Grrr.

She had it now. She gnawed at the stone, a pebble that spoke.

Stop.

Rather than listen, she knocked it off the dresser.

It hit the floor, and the stone popped free.

It rolled, trying to escape.

She soared, the avenging Nefertiti. With great agility, she landed on the stone and grabbed it with her mouth.

She claimed victory and trotted into the room with her servants to show them her triumph.

Only Zach looked as if he needed to defecate, and

his female as if she'd cook Nefertiti like Nonna kept threatening. Joe yelled, "Spit it out."

Did a servant think to order her around?

Nefertiti swallowed it.

The End.

Doubtful, because I do wonder what happens next. Thanks for staying with me thus far on this adventure. ~Eve.

More books in A Lion's Pride:

Need some new shifters to love?

Be sure to visit www.EveLanglais for more books with furry heroes, or sign up for the Eve Langlais newsletter for notification about new stories or specials.